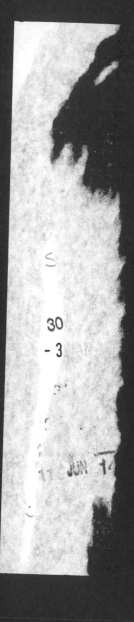

THE MISUNDERSTANDING

IRÈNE NÉMIROVSKY

The Misunderstanding

Translated from the French by Sandra Smith

Chatto & Windus
LONDON

Published by Chatto & Windus 2012

First published in France as *Le Malentendu* in 1926 by *Les Œuvres libres*

2 4 6 8 10 9 7 5 3 1

Copyright © Editions Denoël

Translation copyright © Sandra Smith 2012

The Estate of Irène Némirovsky has asserted her right under the Copyright,
Designs and Patents Act 1988 to be identified as the author of this work

First published in Great Britain in 2012 by
Chatto & Windus
Random House, 20 Vauxhall Bridge Road,
London SW1V 2SA

www.randomhouse.co.uk

Addresses for companies within The Random House Group Limited can be found at:
www.randomhouse.co.uk/offices.htm

The Random House Group Limited Reg. No. 954009

A CIP catalogue record for this book
is available from the British Library

Hardback ISBN 9780701186753

The Random House Group Limited supports The Forest Stewardship Council
(FSC®), the leading international forest certification organisation. Our books
carrying the FSC label are printed on FSC® certified paper. FSC is the only forest
certification scheme endorsed by the leading environmental organisations, including
Greenpeace. Our paper procurement policy can be found at
www.randomhouse.co.uk/environment

Typeset in Fournier MT by Palimpsest Book Production Limited
Falkirk, Stirlingshire

Printed and bound in Great Britain by Clays Ltd, St Ives plc

TRANSLATOR'S NOTE

The French title of this novel – *Le Malentendu* – like many of Némirovsky's titles, presents a challenge to a translator as it embodies many meanings: 'the misunderstanding' as a specific event, or 'the person who is misunderstood' or 'incompatibility' when applied to a couple. Némirovsky's novel explores every aspect of these meanings.

In her first novel as in many of her works, Némirovsky closely examines an extra-marital affair. This recurring theme in her fiction undoubtedly stemmed from her parents' situation. Her mother had numerous lovers, and Némirovsky must have witnessed first-hand the effects of such affairs on a marriage and on her adored father. Even in this early novel, however, she is able to see both sides of the question and alternates between writing from the perspective of the man and the woman.

In the 1920s, when *The Misunderstanding* was published, social attitudes towards marriage were beginning to change and this new thinking is reflected here. But the novel also deals with the effects of the Great War on young men who survived it, as well as with the psychological and economic damage caused by the war to a part of French society: many members of the leisured classes lost their fortunes and were suddenly forced to work for a living. In this novel, most of the problems are caused by the difference in status between Denise Jessaint, 'a young wife doted upon by a husband who earned a lot of money', and Yves Harteloup, formerly wealthy but now forced to work in an office. Némirovsky presents this situation with an ironic perspective: morality isn't the issue, just money. '"When I'm with her," he thought with remarkable irritation, "I always have to be mentally wearing a dinner jacket."'

When reading *The Misunderstanding*, I was struck by the echoes of *Madame Bovary*: both novels explore the thoughts and feelings of bored wives with heightened ideas of romance as they fall passionately in love and enter into affairs. (And Némirovsky did acknowledge Flaubert as an influence.) However, there is a twist in this tale: it is the woman who is wealthy and the man poor. Yves and Denise struggle to overcome their differences as a tribute to their love.

The Misunderstanding was written in 1924 when Irène Némirovsky was barely twenty-one years old, but not published until 1926. It was then reissued in 1930, after the enormous success of the novel *David Golder* had made her famous. Its language, more consciously romantic than in her later work, has the intensity and enthusiasm of youth, but *The Misunderstanding* is an astute, lyrical novel that shows remarkable psychological insight.

Sandra Smith
Cambridge, March 2012

1

Yves was sleeping, like a little boy, soundly, deeply. He had buried his head in the crook of his elbow, instinctively redis-covering, in that intense, trusting sleep of the past, the move-ments and even the smile of a serious, innocent child; he was dreaming of a long beach drenched in sunshine, of the evening sun on the sea, of sunlight through the tamarisk trees.

And yet, it was more than fourteen years since he had been back to Hendaye; arriving after dark the night before, he had caught only glimpses of this enchanting corner of the Basque region: a shadowy abyss full of sounds – the sea – a few lights glimmering through an even darker patch which he guessed was a tamarisk wood and then some other lights at the edge of the waves – the Casino – where only the fishermen's boats used to sway in the past. But the sunlit paradise of his childhood remained unspoiled in his memory and was resurrected in his dreams, down to the tiniest detail, down to the particular scent and taste of the air.

As a child, Yves had spent his most wonderful holidays in Hendaye. There he had savoured long, golden days, as delicious as ripe fruit beneath a sun that to his amazed eyes seemed utterly new, as if it had just been created. Since that time the universe had gradually seemed to lose its bright colours; even the sun had grown dimmer. But the young man still had his vivid, charmed imagination and, in certain dreams, he managed to recapture those childhood impressions in all their original splendour. The mornings that followed such nights seemed tinged by a kind of delicious, enchanted sadness.

On this morning, Yves woke with a start at the stroke of eight, as he always did in Paris. He opened his eyes and started to leap out of bed; but through the slats in the louvred shutters, he saw a shard of light, like a golden arrow, gliding right to his bedside, and at the same time, he heard the soft buzzing that accompanies beautiful summer days in the country mingling with the cries of tennis players and those special, cheerful sounds – bells ringing, footsteps, foreign voices – which, in themselves, are enough to make you realise that you are in a hotel, a large establishment full of idle people without a care in the world.

So Yves went back to bed, smiled, stretched out, enjoying his every exquisite, lazy movement, as if he had rediscovered a sense of luxury. Finally, he reached for the little bell that hung between the brass bars of his bed and rang it. A little while later the waiter came in, carrying a breakfast tray. He opened the shutters and the sun flooded into the room.

'It's a very beautiful day,' Yves said out loud, just as he

had when he was a schoolboy and all his concerns and pleasures depended entirely on the weather. He jumped out of bed and ran barefoot to the window. At first he was disappointed: he had known Hendaye when it was a tiny hamlet of fishermen and smugglers with only two villas, one owned by the writer Pierre Loti, a bit further off to the left, near the Bidassoa river, and the other owned by his parents, to the right, at the very spot where now stood twenty-odd houses in mock Basque style. He saw that a sea wall planted with sparse trees had been laid out behind the beach, where cars could park. He looked away, sulking. Why had they spoiled this sacred corner of the world that he so loved for its very simplicity, its peaceful charm? He stood next to the open window and little by little, just as you begin to recognise a face that has changed over the years by its smile and the expression in its eyes and so gradually recall the features you once loved, in the same way Yves rediscovered with a deep sense of pleasure the lines, the colours, the contour of the mountains, the glistening water of the bay, the light, swaying fronds of the tamarisks. And when he sensed once more the scent of cinnamon and orange blossom carried in by the winds from Andalusia, he made peace with the passing of time; he smiled, and the lightness of spirit he had felt in the past returned to fill his heart.

Reluctantly, he turned away from the window and went over to the bathroom; painted in high-gloss lacquer with white tiles, it gleamed in the dazzling sunlight. Yves drew the curtains; they were made of lace, decorated with intricate designs, so immediately the same patterns swept across the floor, in a light, shimmering, delicate layer that flickered each time the sea breeze rustled the curtains. Yves watched with delight the play between light and shadow; he remembered that this used to be his favourite pastime as a little boy. And every time he recognised one of his childhood traits in the man he had become, he experienced the kind of emotion you feel when looking at old photographs, along with a vague sense of anguish.

He raised his eyes and saw himself in the mirror. That day he felt his spirits so akin to the way he used to feel as a child on those beautiful mornings that his reflection caused him painful surprise. It was a face in its thirties, so weary, so lacklustre, with its muddy complexion and that slight bitter grimace at the corner of his mouth, blue eyes that seemed to have faded, dark eyelids that had lost their silky lashes . . . The face of a young man, true, but already altered, sculpted by the hand of time that gently, pitilessly, etched a delicate maze of lines in the fresh smooth surface of his youthful skin, the first mocking sign of the wrinkles to come. Yves passed a hand over his forehead where his hair was already thinning at the temples; then in an unconscious gesture, he rubbed the place where his hair had grown back coarser, the scar from his last wound – a shell that had exploded and almost killed him in Belgium, near that grim section of charred wall standing among dead trees . . .

But the waiter who came to remove the breakfast tray tore him away from thoughts that were insidiously depressing him, like the effect on certain summer days when a sky that looks too blue grows imperceptibly darker until it takes on the grey-black colour of a storm. Yves slipped on his espadrilles and swimming trunks, threw a bathrobe over his shoulder and went down to the beach.

2

Yves lay down in the warm sand that crunched between his bare feet, closed his eyes, stretched out and remained perfectly still, relishing the feel of the burning sun on every inch of his body, on his face that he turned up towards the intense light of the August sky, white with heat, a singular sensation of silent, perfect, almost primeval joy.

All around him men and women, young and beautiful for the most part, scantily clad and unbelievably suntanned, moved lithely past. Others lay about in groups, drying their wet bodies in the sun, as he was; there were teenagers, stripped to the waist, playing with beach balls at the water's edge; they ran along the bright sand, like shadow puppets. Tired from having stayed in the water too long, Yves closed his eyes; the brutal midday light pierced his closed eyelids, plunging him into burning darkness where enormous suns floated past, opaque and fiery. The air was filled with the resounding noise of the waves as they beat against the sand with a sound of powerful wings. A child's shrill laughter interrupted Yves's reverie; frantic little feet ran right up to him and he was hit by a handful of sand.

He sat up and heard a woman's voice: 'Francette, for goodness sake,' she cried, outraged, 'Francette, will you please behave yourself and come over here right this minute!'

Yves, now completely awake, sat up cross-legged and opened his eyes wide; he saw the pretty silhouette of a shapely woman in a black swimsuit who was being pulled away by a very little girl. The child couldn't have been more than two or three years old; she was a sturdy, funny little thing with a mass of blonde hair that the sun had bleached to the colour of straw and a small round body that was almost as dark as an African's.

Yves saw them walk off towards the sea. He watched them for a long time, with a vague sense of pleasure due equally to the child as to her pretty mother. He hadn't seen the woman's face, but her body had the shape of a ravishing little statue. He couldn't help but smile as he thought of the many circumstances that would have had to coincide in Paris to allow him such a vision, one that seemed so natural here at the seaside. Seeing her there, all suntanned and rosy, with the curves and lines of her body that he could make out under her swimsuit, made him feel as if this woman belonged to him somehow, unbeknownst to her, because to him she was as naked as if she were standing in front of her lover. That was perhaps why he felt a very slight, very fleeting sense of anguish as soon as he lost sight of her among the crowd of bathers: it was one of those

7

strange moments of regret: when set against intense despair, though, it is no more than a pinprick compared to a knife wound.

He stretched out on his side with a sudden vague sense of uneasiness; he began to play absent-mindedly with a handful of golden sand, which he let flow through his fingers like a strand of fine hair, silky and irritating. Then he looked out at the sea once more in the hope of seeing the woman, as yet only half-glimpsed, coming out of the water. Female shapes, deeply tanned and rosy, passed in front of him; he was getting more and more agitated, and still he couldn't find the woman he had seen earlier. Finally he spotted her, thanks to the child who caught his attention because she was crying and stamping her feet: the poor little girl had swallowed some bitter, salty water which had surely caused her noisy protest. Her mother laughed a little, called her a 'silly little thing' and then consoled her; suddenly she reached down, picked her up, sat her on her shoulders and started to run. Yves could clearly see the outline of her breasts, firm and very shapely; her waist was supple and strong, the kind of figure belonging to young women who had never worn a corset, women who walked a lot and have always danced; she looked both energetic and delicate, and vaguely reminded him of the figure of a Greek woman running, without bending her body, beneath the weight of a large clay jug held high on her shoulder. This was how she carried her beautiful child, and she was both very natural and very beautiful against this natural and beautiful background. Yves pushed himself up on to his elbows with an odd sense of anxiety: he wanted to get a better look at her when she passed him; he wanted to see every detail of her face and finally, he did: it was suntanned and almost as bronzed as her little girl's, with a round, dimpled chin, moist, red parted lips that must have smelled of salt and sea spray, an open, rather stern expression that you find in children and, sometimes, in very young women. Then he saw her short black hair, dishevelled by the biting sea breeze over a smooth little forehead; those locks – so messy and unruly – resembled the marble curls on Greek statues of young boys. She was really very pretty. She had already disappeared inside a beach tent. He was disappointed, because he hadn't had a chance to see the colour of her eyes.

A few seconds later he climbed back up the garden of the hotel; the fresh air and sun made him feel rather dizzy and gave him a slight, but persistent, annoying headache. He walked slowly and half closed his eyes but couldn't manage to blot out the awful light that seemed to filter through his eyelids, making it difficult to see: he was used to the pale colours of the Paris sky. He went into the foyer and there, the first thing he saw was the little girl who had thrown sand at him; she was bouncing up and down, laughing loudly, on the knee of a man dressed all in white. Yves looked at him and thought he recognised him; he asked the bellboy who operated the lift if he knew the man's name.

'Monsieur Jessaint,' the boy replied.

'I do know him,' Yves thought.

He didn't doubt for a moment that the man was the

husband of the beautiful creature he had seen on the beach; but instead of being pleased at this bit of fortuitous luck that would allow him to meet her in a quick, simple and convenient way, he grumbled with all the illogical reasoning that comes so naturally to men: 'Damn! More people from back there . . . Can't I even have a few peaceful weeks to myself?'

3

Yves Harteloup was born in 1890, at the height of the '*fin de siècle*', that divine, decadent era when there were still men in Paris who had absolutely nothing to do, when people were doggedly perverse and proud of their depravity, a time when, for most people, life flowed by like a narrow and calm little stream whose end could be envisaged from its beginnings, a smooth and even course whose length could more or less be predicted.

Yves's father was a member of a 'special club', as they were called at the time, a pure-bred Parisian who led the leisured yet bustling existence of all his peers; he had two passions, though: women and horses. Both had given him the same heady sensation of wild abandon and danger. Thanks to horses, and thanks to women, he could say, as he lay dying, that he had never left Paris except to go to Nice or Trouville, having never known any world other than the grands boulevards, the horse races and the Bois de Boulogne. Having limited his attention to women's eyes and his desires to their lips, when dying, he could tell the priest, who was promising him eternal life: 'What use is that to me? All I want is peace. I've experienced everything else.'

Yves was eighteen when his father died. He clearly remembered his soft hands, his tender, slightly mocking smile, the faint, annoying perfume that always followed him, as if the folds of his clothing had retained the sweet smell of all the women he'd made love to. Yves looked like him: he had the same bright, striking eyes and beautiful hands designed to be idle and make love; but his father's eyes had been so sharp, so passionately alive, while in his son they were sometimes lifeless, so full of world-weariness and apprehension, as dark as deep water . . .

Yves also remembered his mother extremely well, even though he had lost her when he was very young; every morning his governess took him to see her in her room, while her hair was being done. She wore delicate peignoirs with frills and flounces of lace that made the sound of birds taking flight when she walked. He even recalled the black satin corsets that shaped her pretty, slim figure into the hourglass silhouette demanded by the fashion of the day, and her red hair and rosy complexion.

He'd had the happy childhood of a little rich boy who was healthy and pampered. His parents loved him, worried about him, and since they believed they could foresee the future life he would surely lead – free, wealthy, never needing to work – they made an effort to instil in him, from an early age, a taste for beauty, a way of thinking that dignified life, as well as a thousand subtle nuances of elegance and luxury that enhance that existence and give rise to unsurpassed pleasure. So Yves grew up learning to love beautiful things and how to spend money, how to dress, how to ride a horse, to fence and also – thanks to his father's discreet example – how to regard women as the only worthwhile worldly possession, how to see sensuality as an art and life as elegant, light-hearted and beautiful, from which the wise man should take only joy.

At the age of eighteen, having finished his studies, Yves found himself an orphan and quite a wealthy one. Forced into relative solitude because he was in mourning, he began to get bored, vaguely thought about starting a university degree, then got the idea to travel, for he was different from his father in that respect, different from his father's entire generation in that the world was not limited to the Avenue de l'Opéra and the Sentier de la Vertu in the Bois de Boulogne; he had a keen sense of curiosity about foreign lands which his father had mockingly labelled 'romantic'. So Yves spent several months in England, dreamed of a trip to Japan that never materialised, visited some small dead old German villages, spent a few wonderful, peaceful days in Siena and the spring in Spain, inspired to go there by his happiest childhood memories of Hendaye, on the Spanish border, in an ancient house that belonged to his parents, and where he and his governess used to be sent to spend the summer holidays. He travelled constantly for a little more than two years, finally returning to Paris at the beginning of 1911. He settled there once and for all, arranging to do his military service in Versailles. The next two or three passed years quickly and calmly. He remembered them now as one recalls certain springtimes: brief, full of sunshine and fleeting love affairs, which all seem so empty yet enchanting. And then, abruptly, war exploded right into his existence, like a thunderbolt straight out of a blue sky.

1914: his departure, initial enthusiasm, the horrors of death. 1915: cold, hunger, mud in the trenches, death becoming a familiar companion who walks alongside you and sleeps in your dugout. 1916: more cold, filth, death. 1917: exhaustion, resignation, death . . . A long, long nightmare . . . Some of those who had survived, the calm middle-class men, had returned unchanged; they slid back into their former way of life, their former state of mind, as they slid back into their old slippers. Others, the passionate men, had returned to society with their outrage, their fervour, their tormented desires. Still others, like Yves, had simply come home exhausted. At first they believed it would pass, that the memories of those dark hours would fade as life became peaceful, normal, serene; they believed they would wake up one beautiful morning as energetic, joyful and young as before. But time passed, and 'it' remained, like some slow-working poison. 'It': that strange faraway look which had seen every sort of human horror, every type of misery, every fear; a disregard for life and the bitter desire for its basest joys, its most carnal pleasures; idleness, because the only work they had done back there, for so many years, was to sit by, with folded arms, waiting for death; and a kind of bitter hostility towards others, all the others, because they hadn't suffered, because they hadn't seen . . . Many men had returned with these or similar thoughts; many had continued to exist, like Lazarus risen, walking among the living, arms outstretched, steps hindered by a shroud, pupils dilated in desolate terror.

It was only in 1919 that Yves, who had been wounded three times and awarded the Croix de Guerre, returned to Paris for good. He began to put his affairs in order, to calculate what remained of his fortune. His inheritance had been divided into two parts and held in trust by a lawyer until he reached his majority. The portion he had inherited from his mother had been invested in a factory belonging to his maternal uncle, a fabulously wealthy industrialist. Nothing left of that: his uncle had died penniless in 1915. As for his father's money, it had been used before the war to buy foreign stocks and shares, Russian and German for the most part. In the end, Yves found himself with an income that was sufficient to pay for his cigarettes and taxis. He would have to work for a living. Later on, he could never think back on those years without a shiver down his spine. This young man, who for four years had been a kind of hero, was cowardly when faced with the daily grind, the need to work, the petty tyranny of existence. He undoubtedly could have taken a rich wife, as many others did, by marrying the daughter of some nouveau riche family or a wealthy American; but this went against his upbringing which had given him all the scruples and sensitivity that are a luxury, just like others, but more burdensome, along with certain principles that furnish a conscience similar to a Gothic chair: very hard with a high back, very beautiful and very uncomfortable. Yves had finally found a post in the administrative offices of a large agency specialising in international news – two thousand five hundred francs per month, better than he could have hoped for.

Since 1920 – it was now August 1924 – Yves had led the life of an employee, a life he hated in the way certain small boys who are very lazy and very sensitive hate boarding school. He had kept his old apartment; it was full of memories, flowers, beautiful objects lovingly displayed. Every morning at eight o'clock, when he had to get out of bed, quickly dress and leave its shadowy warmth for the brutally cold street and his hostile, bare office where the entire day was spent giving and receiving orders, writing and talking to people, Yves felt the same despair, the same hateful, vain impulse to rebel, a horrible, black, crushing boredom. He was neither ambitious nor motivated; he carried out his duties with care, almost the way a pupil prepares his lessons for school.

The very idea that he might be good at business or might fight to try to become rich again never even crossed his mind. As the son and grandson of rich men, idle men, he suffered from his lack of comfort, the inability to be carefree, the way other people suffer from hunger or cold. Gradually he grew used to his life, because people eventually get used to everything, more or less, but his grim resignation weighed heavily upon him. The days dragged on, each the same, bringing with them, come the evening, a feeling of extreme weariness, headaches, a bitter and unhealthy need for solitude. He would eat quickly at a restaurant, or sitting by the fire with his dog Pierrot at his feet, a curly white Spitz that looked like a china figurine of a sheep, and he would go to bed early because cabarets and dance halls were expensive, because he had to get up early the next day. He had mistresses, affairs that lasted two or three months at the most, quickly begun and quickly ended: he very soon got bored with them. He changed women often because he concluded that only the first encounter was worth anything: he was an expert at the essentially modern art of 'dropping women': he knew how to get rid of them gently. Sometimes, after he'd just broken off with one of them, he felt as if a burden had been lifted from his shoulders and he would remember his father, who believed he could find the meaning of life in a woman's eyes, her breasts, those brief explosions of pleasure. A woman . . . To Yves, a woman was nothing more than a pretty, useful object: firstly, he'd had so many since the war, they were so easy . . . and then because really . . . no, no, he did his best to look deep into those loving, lying eyes but never found that intimate essential thrill, that elusive glimpse of the unknown that his father believed he had attained and which Yves too, perhaps, was searching for blindly, without realising it. And he thought that for someone who had looked deep into the eyes of dying men, someone who had fallen in battle, wounded, someone who had opened his eyes wide in despair to catch a glimpse of sky before he died, for a man like that a woman held no secret, no mystery, no other attractions except her willingness, her beauty, her youth. Love . . . love must be a feeling of peace, of calm, of infinite serenity . . . Love must be so soothing . . . if it even existed . . .

4

Every summer Yves got a few weeks off and, since he led a very frugal life all winter, he could allow himself to spend his holidays as he pleased. This year he had gone back to Hendaye, moved by the idea of seeing once more the enchanting beach of his childhood, and because he thought that Hendaye held fewer temptations than other places while still being close to Biarritz and Saint Sebastian, two of the most attractive cities on the cosmopolitan circuit. Besides, he loved both the wild, free waves and the dazzling light of the Basque country. And the idle, easy life of the best hotels gave him the same pleasant sensation of renewed comfort that you feel when you sink into a bathtub full of warm water after a long train journey.

The day after arriving, Yves left his room at two o'clock; he had taken his time to dress meticulously; he finished lunch almost alone in the immense dining room. In spite of the lowered canvas awnings that shaded the large bay windows, the sun spread through the dining room in waves: gleaming, tawny-coloured, like a fabulous mane of hair. Yves forced himself to resist the childish temptation that came over him to wave his fingers through the golden rays that danced over the tablecloth and cutlery, and lit up his glass of vintage Burgundy as if it were filled with blood and rubies. Nearby, a few Spanish families were finishing their meal, jabbering at the tops of their voices. The women were heavy-set and losing their looks; the young men were very handsome. But almost all of them had wonderful eyes, fiery and lush as velvet, and as he watched them Yves recalled how close Spain was and dreamed of going there in October, to see the pink houses and patios with water fountains again. But, just in time, his hazy daydream was brutally invaded by the annoying reminder of the date when his holidays would end, just as if it were a figure representing the value of the peseta during this month of August in the year of our Lord 1924, so, sadly but sensibly, he looked away, letting his gaze wander off towards the Pyrenees and back to the fat, juicy pear he was peeling. He finished eating it, then went out on to the terrace.

A few people were sitting around wicker tables in groups, drinking coffee and reading the newspapers from Paris or Madrid. Some musicians were lazily tuning up their instruments on a small platform. In the garden energetic teenagers were already playing tennis. The sea breeze filled the large cloth awnings, making them flap like the sails of a boat. Yves walked over to the balustrade to look out at the sea: he never grew tired of it.

He heard someone call out his name: 'How are you, Harteloup? Have you been here long?'

He turned round and recognised Jessaint. Next to him, in a rocking chair, the young woman he had glimpsed earlier was swaying back and forth. She was dressed all in white, with bare legs and no hat, and wore sandals tied with ribbons on her delicate feet. Beside her, her little girl was romping about on the warm paving stones of the terrace.

'Do you know my wife?' Jessaint asked. 'Denise, this is Monsieur Harteloup.'

Yves bowed; then he replied to the first question he had been asked: 'I just got here yesterday. That should be obvious,' he added, smiling as he stretched out his pale Parisian hands.

The young woman began to laugh. 'You're right! We're all as dark as Africans here . . .'

Then she looked more closely at Yves and continued: 'Am I wrong or . . . was it you my little girl threw sand at earlier, on the beach? I should have apologised right away; but I preferred to pretend I thought you were asleep . . . I was embarrassed to have such a naughty little girl,' she added, pulling the child close; her daughter raised her round, happy face and looked at her.

Yves put on a gruff voice. 'So, Mademoiselle, you're the one who tortures poor little boys who have never done a thing to you?'

The child burst out laughing as she hid her head between her mother's knees.

'She seems to be in a good mood,' said Yves.

'She's impossible,' said her mother, but with much pride in her eyes.

She lifted the tiny round chin buried in her dress. 'Well, you must forgive us, even though we are very mischievous and very naughty, because we are still very young, isn't that right, Mademoiselle Francette?' she said. 'We're not even two and a half yet.'

'Certainly not,' said Yves, 'I won't forgive her.'

He took the pretty little girl in his arms and started throwing her up in the air and catching her; she kicked her bare legs with all her might and squealed with laughter. When Yves pretended to put her down on the ground she begged: 'Again, again, please, Monsieur'; and Yves, delighted to have a game with this rosy, tanned little bundle, started all over again, even more vigorously than before. Both of them were disappointed to say goodbye when her nanny came to take Mademoiselle Francette to the beach.

'Do you like children?' asked Jessaint after the reluctant infant was taken away.

'I adore them, especially when they are good-looking and healthy and always laughing, like your little girl.'

'She's not always like that,' said Denise, smiling, 'especially here. The sea goes to her head. She goes from laughter to tears so suddenly and with such ease that sometimes I despair.'

'What do you call her?'

'Francette, France, because she was born on the anniversary of the Armistice.'

'It's funny that you like children . . .' said Jessaint. 'I'm crazy about my daughter, it's true, but I can't stand other people's children. They make a noise and are deadly boring.'

'Well, what about yours?' Denise protested. 'She makes more noise than an entire school all by herself!'

'First of all, you're exaggerating . . . And besides, she's mine, as you said, and especially, yours,' he concluded, lightly kissing his wife's hand.

Yves looked at him and saw that his face lit up with affection when he spoke to Denise. Jessaint noticed the keen look the young man shot at them; he was afraid that Yves might think such effusiveness was in bad taste.

'You must think me foolish . . .' he said, somewhat embarrassed, 'it's just that I'm going away, so I'm feeling rather emotional . . .'

'Ah, so you're going away?'

'Yes, to London . . . for a few weeks . . . I'm leaving tonight.'

Then, feeling guilty for talking too much about himself and his family, he asked: 'And what about you, my friend, what have you been up to?'

Yves made a vague gesture.

Jessaint continued to explain to his wife: 'Harteloup and I were at the Saints-Anges Hospital together, in that horrible, gloomy little village in Belgium whose name I forget . . .'

'Wassin . . . or Lieuwassin?'

'Lieuwassin . . . that's it . . . he was badly smashed up, poor man . . .'

'I was shot through the left lung,' said Yves, 'but it's healed now.'

'I'm so glad, really glad . . . My leg is still painful; I can't ride any more.'

'Have you seen each other since then?' asked Denise.

'Yes, occasionally at the Haguets' and also on the rue Bassano, that's right, isn't it? At Louis de Brémont's place? But I didn't know you were married, Jessaint.'

'I wasn't at the time . . . just engaged. Since we got married we rarely go out. I travel a lot for work.'

'I know,' said Yves. 'I've heard about your invention.'

He was talking about a device that could capture and recycle the smoke from factory chimneys, which had earned the young engineer Jessaint a huge fortune during the war and a great deal of fame.

Jessaint blushed slightly; he had a kind face, even though it was somewhat simple with rugged features, but lit by his very soft, very clear blue eyes.

The maître d' had just brought the coffee, so Denise poured it out; the sunlight shimmered on the downy hair of her bare arm; she had the serious smile of a statuette. Then she crossed her hands behind her neck, closed her eyes and started gently swaying back and forth in her rocking chair, while the men continued talking in low voices about the war, about the people who had come back and the ones who hadn't.

A little while later she interrupted them: 'Excuse me . . . Can you tell me what time it is?'

'It's nearly four o'clock, Madame.'

'Oh, then I really should go and get dressed . . . Are we still going to Biarritz to buy your trunk, Jacques?'

'Yes.'

'Well,' said Yves, 'I'm going to have another swim.'

'Aren't you afraid you'll tire yourself out?'

'Absolutely not, I could live in the water!'

They walked off together while Jessaint stayed on the terrace to finish his coffee. Yves watched the young woman in white as she walked in front of him. Against the dazzling sunlight, her black curls were light and bluish, like smoke rings from oriental cigarettes. At the foot of the stairs she turned round and smiled.

'Goodbye, Monsieur, I'm sure I'll see you again soon . . .'

She shook his hand. Her gaze was beautiful, frank, direct, something he had already noticed about her and which he liked. Then she walked away, going through the rotating door of the hotel as Yves made his way slowly down to the beach.

5

The next day at siesta time he saw her again on the warm beach. Jessaint had gone to London as he had said he would. Yves walked over and stroked little France's damp blonde hair, then spoke to her mother about her husband and the friends you discover you have in common as soon as you take the trouble to ask.

He saw her later in the restaurant and noticed their tables were next to each other; he spotted her again in the foyer where she was reading the papers. And so on . . . every day, at every hour of the day, from then on, he would run into her. It was hardly surprising: Hendaye is a very small place and neither of them left Hendaye. Denise didn't like being far from her daughter: she had the worrying nature and anxious imagination of a true mother. Yves was soothed by this charming, regular life that flew by with the unusual speed of certain happy daydreams . . . luminous mornings, long, lazy days in the sun, a brief moment of dusk followed by those Spanish nights that carry the sweet scents of Andalusia back out to sea . . .

To Yves, the presence of Denise seemed as natural and strangely precious as the presence of the ocean. Her feminine silhouette glided among the swaying tamarisk trees like a graceful shadow, born of the sun and the shade. She no longer surprised Yves just as the crashing sound of the waves filled both his wakeful nights and his dreams with brash colours, wild music, which he no longer noticed because he had grown used to them. Denise's beauty left him calm and impassive; even though she ran along the beach in her swim-suit, half-naked, every morning, with the serene lack of modesty you find in very young, very beautiful creatures, Yves was not troubled by desire: he did not experience the arousal, the burning curiosity that plagues men when they first begin to fall in love. She was pretty and, more important, she was wholesome and modest, and her simplicity, her energy, charmed Yves in a way he almost failed to notice. He didn't wonder whether she was an honest woman, if she had one or several lovers. He didn't undress her with his eyes. Why should he? She had no secrets and, because of that, there was no mystery about her. When she was with him he didn't think about her. But wasn't she always with him? In the morning, when he first saw her, he felt happy: to him, was she not the symbol, the visible representation of these joyful holidays? When he had been in Hendaye as a schoolboy, every evening he would see two women pass by on the pier; two Spanish women who wore black mantillas . . . they spoke a coarse, throaty language that he couldn't understand. He couldn't see their faces in the darkness, but when the bright beam from the lighthouse swept over them they were suddenly lit up, almost too brightly, as if they were standing in a spotlight. Then they would fade into the distance, their skirts swaying.

Yves had never spoken a word to them; later on he thought they must have been maids in the hotel. They weren't beautiful, and even if he was vaguely in love with them, as you are at fifteen, he was certainly more smitten with the daughter of the guard, his first mistress, and the little American he kissed on the lips behind the bathing huts. He had forgotten about those girls, though, and when he thought back to that summer of his adolescence, those two foreign women chatting in their strange language, with their swaying skirts and black mantillas in their hair, immediately came to mind . . . In the same way, he told himself, that if he later saw Denise again on some street in Paris, he would remember in incredible detail, all the wild splendour of a summer's day, the warm, golden beach that curved along the Bidassoa river. Music has the same power to evoke days gone by, thought Yves, very simple music preferably, and certain women's faces as well.

6

One day Denise wasn't at the beach. Yves did not notice at first; he went into the water, as always, swam for a long time, his eyes dazzled by the glittering flecks of gold that dance between the waves. He lay down in the sand in his usual spot, very close to Denise's beach tent. The young woman was not there. Little Francette, in her bathing suit, made sand pies and then immediately demolished them, bashing them with her spade with wild, destructive energy. Her nanny was reading.

Yves tossed and turned, sighing nervously, like a sleeping dog having a dream. He felt anxious but couldn't understand why; he was having difficulty breathing and he could hear his heart beating faster. 'I stayed in the water too long,' he thought. He raised himself up on one elbow and waved at the child to call her over: she recognised him, started to laugh, stood up, took a few steps forward, then turned away and ran off with the inexplicable instinct children have for teasing. He lay back down, so frustrated that he bit his lips in irritation. He stubbornly continued to try to discover the cause of his nervousness by looking for natural, physical reasons: it was hot, the sun weighed heavily down on his shoulders like a leaden cloak; every now and then a burning breeze scattered sand over his legs, tickling his bare skin in a way he found unbearable. He didn't consciously wonder where Madame Jessaint was yet answered this unspoken question with vague, hypocritical replies: 'She'll be here . . . she's been delayed . . . maybe she's not well . . . she's not going swimming but she'll come down to the beach when her child goes in the water . . . it's not that late yet . . .' And he turned over again on the warm sand, like a sick man in his bed, unable to lie still, not actually unhappy, but feeling exactly what the English call 'uncomfortable', without managing to understand why. All the while, the sun rose in the sky above his head; more and more people left the beach; only the half-naked young boys playing beach ball at the water's edge remained. Eventually they too left. The lifeguard and his assistants passed by, dragging the lifeboat they stored away at lunchtime; their wet, muscular, tanned arms strained like cables as they slowly walked away. The flat, deserted beach seemed endless, dazzling in the midday sun. Yves remained there, motionless, his head heavy and his throat tight with emotion. Suddenly he leaped up, told himself he was a fool; she must not have been feeling well so hadn't come to the beach that morning, but she would surely come down for lunch! She wasn't so ill, he reasoned, that she would have to stay in bed on such a beautiful day: but it must be terribly late; by the time he'd shaved and dressed she'd be gone. Hastily throwing his robe over one shoulder, he ran quickly towards the hotel.

Twenty minutes later he was in the lobby, but Denise was not there; her table was laid but untouched. Yves thought his lamb chop was burned, his peas undercooked, his coffee undrinkable and the waiters incompetent. He complained bitterly to the maître d' and asked for the wine waiter to be sent over so he could tell him that in any cheap restaurant in Paris the house red was better than his Corton 1898, a remark that almost made the dignified man burst into tears.

Without even touching the peach he'd put on his plate, Yves threw down his napkin and went out on to the terrace. In Denise's chair, a serious-looking Mademoiselle Francette was rocking back and forth, wearing a short linen dress, as blue as the sky. When she saw the young man walking towards her, she jumped up, threw her arms round him and swung from his neck.

'Sing "This is the way the ladies ride" for me, please, Monsieur Loulou!'

She couldn't pronounce 'Monsieur Harteloup' as her mother did, so she had given her friend a nickname. Yves sat her on his knee while humming the refrain of the English nursery rhyme.

'Tell me, Fanchon,' he said, 'your mama isn't ill, is she?' and his flat tone of voice sounded strange even to him.

'No,' said Francette, and she started shaking her head from left to right and right to left, like some Chinese toy. 'No.'

'Where is she?'

'She went away.'

'Will she be gone long?'

'Oh, *I* don't know!'

'Of course you do, just think,' Yves gently encouraged her. 'Your mama told you before she left, I bet . . . And when she was kissing you goodbye this morning, didn't she say: "Goodbye, my darling, be a good girl and I'll be back in a day . . . or two"? Didn't she say that?'

'No,' said Francette, 'she didn't say anything.'

Then she thought for a moment and added: 'You see, I was still asleep when she came in to kiss me this morning before she went away.'

Yves was tempted to ask the nanny, but didn't dare: he feared arousing any suspicion, even though there was nothing to be suspicious about for heaven's sake! He set the little girl down on the ground and walked away.

Where could she have gone? For how long? It was so absurd: he knew perfectly well she couldn't be gone for long because she'd left Francette in Hendaye. Perhaps Denise had gone to Biarritz to do some shopping? But then, who was she meeting for lunch? Friends? Which friends? For the first time his exasperated mind began to roam wildly through the world that belonged to Denise; unknown like everyone's, but whose mystery, until that moment, had not caused him to suffer. Perhaps she was having an intimate lunch with someone? He pictured all the restaurants he knew in Biarritz, one after the other, from the most expensive hotels down to the inns on the outskirts, hidden away in the countryside. Blind rage swept through him. It took all his strength of will to calm himself down, but he was trembling, ashamed, unable to concentrate. Then he went down to the beach and started walking, just walking without knowing where he was going. Maybe her friends had taken her on an outing? Oh, friends he needn't worry about, relatives perhaps . . . She hadn't said anything about it to him the day before, but they didn't normally say very much to each other . . . Yes, that must be it . . . An outing . . . some of them can last for quite a while, two or three days . . . But if she'd gone to Spain or to Lourdes, she could be away from Hendaye for a week . . . away from him . . . Seven days, seven mornings, seven long evenings . . . it may seem like nothing, but it's horrible . . . Perhaps her husband had suddenly called her to London? An accident, illness, who knows? She wouldn't come back . . . The nanny would take Francette to England . . . He began to panic, as if someone had told him that Denise had died. He threw himself to the ground. The sun beat down on him brutally; he buried his hands deeper into the sand to feel the moist freshness of the sea water; its sharp coolness made him shiver; he stood up.

He flew into a rage, furious, began lashing out at himself: 'She's gone . . . so what? I'm not in love with her, am I? Am I? So what then . . . ? I couldn't care less . . . I'm an idiot, a complete idiot.'

He passionately believed what he was thinking, but his lips were trembling and he automatically repeated again and again what he had first said: 'She's gone . . . that's all there is to it . . . She's gone.'

He walked back to the hotel and went to bed. For a long time he lay there without moving, his head turned to the wall, just the way he used to when he was a little boy and was feeling sad.

At five o'clock he went out, walked aimlessly around the terrace, paced up and down the garden several times, then, defeated, set off for the Casino, although she rarely went there. Young men, young women, their heads bare, danced on a platform set on pillars above the water. The endless movement of the sea around the pillars, the canopy flapping in the wind, the creaking noises and the smell of the salty sea air, everything made you feel as if you were on a boat moored in port. Yves thought he would enjoy the solace; he ordered a cocktail, drank only half of it and left.

At seven o'clock the sea was growing pale beneath the sun; very small pink clouds formed delicate coils in the sky. Yves listened to the sea; it had always consoled him and tonight he would entrust his poor, weary body to its core.

He took off his clothes and walked slowly towards the Bidassoa river. The sea wall was carefully kept in good condition for several metres, but further along it was riddled with fine sand; there was no railing any more; little bushes bristling with thorns sprung up between the stones. Then the sea wall suddenly stopped. Yves kept on walking until he got to the beach; it was a narrow arc, its shape carved out by the water. To the left was the bay; to the right the sea, and linking them was the Bidassoa, so calm that it did not even shimmer, and as pale as the watery reflection of the pallid sky. On the other side was Spain.

Yves sat down, folding his legs under him, his chin resting on his closed fist. There wasn't a soul in sight. It was strange . . . The crashing of the waves did not disturb the magical silence of the evening. A small boat passed by, gliding along the river from one coast to the other, from France to Spain, without a sound. A golden glow, more delicate than the midday light, washed over the mountain tops, but shadows were already spreading across the valleys. Yves's anger suddenly began to ebb and an inexplicable feeling of sadness rushed through him.

Night was falling very quickly; in the solitary darkness the sea seemed further away again, vast in its primal majesty. Yves felt very small, lost in the immensity of this ancient earth. He thought about himself, about his failed life. He was unhappy, he was alone, he was poor. From now on his days would be spent without joy. No one needed him. Life was hard, so hard . . . He wanted to cry; through one final desperate effort of masculine pride he held back his tears, but they welled up in his heart, rose to his throat, choking him.

A lovely dusk, hazy blue and pink, settled over the countryside, growing gradually darker. Church bells were ringing. On the opposite shore you could see the lights of Fuenterrabia: the windows in houses, bright tramways, the outline of its streets; only the large square tower of the old church looked dark and bleak. The bells rang out slowly, as if they were weary, discouraged, sad. And in the mountains farmhouses lit up, one by one, like stars. Night had fallen.

All around Yves a mysterious world was coming to life: murmurings, humming, the sounds of a swarm of living creatures, invisible insects that live in the sand and are heard only at night. Yves listened, trembling with inexplicable fear. Then, suddenly, overwhelmed by his sadness, he burst into tears. He put his head in his hands and cried – for the first time in so very many years – he cried like a child, letting the tears rush down his face.

'Is that you?' a voice he knew asked rather hesitantly. 'You're going to catch cold; it's so late . . .'

Yves raised his head and opened his eyes wide. It was Denise, her dress a glimmer of white in the dark night.

'I'll have to scold you,' she continued softly. 'You have no more sense than my daughter . . . Do people go swimming this late at night?'

'Is it that late?' Yves mumbled.

He had instinctively stood up.

'It's after nine.'

'Oh! Is it really . . . I . . . I didn't know . . . No, truly, I'd forgotten . . .'

'Good Lord,' she said anxiously, 'what's wrong?'

She tried to look at his face but it was far too dark. Yet she could tell he had been crying from his voice, from the sobs he was barely holding back . . . Instinctively her soft, maternal hands reached out towards him, hands that could console, could bring such peace. He stood before her, trembling, and lowered his head. He was crying softly, without shame; he felt as if all the blood and poison from a very old wound were flowing away with those tears. He savoured the taste of salt and water on his lips with a unique feeling of sensuality, a taste he'd forgotten long ago.

'What is it?' she whispered again, her voice choked with emotion. 'What's wrong?'

'Nothing,' he said, 'nothing.'

Suddenly she wondered if she had perhaps interrupted a moment of private grief. She started to walk away; in an instant he was by her side. She could feel Yves's warm hand on her bare arm.

'Don't go, please don't go . . .' he stammered, not quite knowing what he was saying.

Then, all at once, sounding almost angry, he shouted: 'Where were you all day?'

Taken aback, all she could do was reply meekly: 'I was in Biarritz.'

Then, with a strange insight into how much he had been suffering, she added: 'My mother lives there . . .'

A short silence fell between them. In the dim light from the stars she could see his tormented face, his harsh yet tender mouth, his pleading eyes.

Suddenly she put her arms round his neck. They did not kiss; they simply stood there, holding each other tightly, overcome with emotion, their hearts pounding with heavy, exquisite sadness.

Instinctively, in a timeless gesture, he buried his head in her shoulder as she leaned towards him and she stroked his forehead, in silence but with a sudden desire to cry herself.

All around them the waves from the sea flowed wild and free; the wind from Spain carried with it the faint sound of music; the ancient earth quivered, alive with the mysterious, nebulous life of the night.

Slowly, reluctantly, they let go of one another. He stood before her, half-naked; her eyes had grown accustomed to the faint light that fell from the sky so she could just about make out the shape of his tall, masculine body in nothing but his swimming trunks. She'd seen him like this a hundred times; but tonight, like Eve, she realised for the first time that he was naked. Then she felt ashamed and afraid, as if she were a young girl. She pushed him away gently, vanished up a sand dune and into the night.

He didn't dare go back to the hotel without his clothes; he remembered he had slept on the beach many times as a child. Wrapping himself in his robe, he huddled in the sand and fell asleep: it was a light, feverish sleep, interrupted by dreams, full of the sounds and scents of the sea.

7

That night, as every night, Denise went and sat next to the little bed where Francette slept. Thumb in her mouth, Francette was off in the land of the sandman; in the soft light her tiny neck had deep creases of pink skin, as if she were wearing a necklace; she looked exactly like a fledgling, fragile and warm, nestled in the gentle heat of its feathers.

Denise leaned over to see her better. With unusual clarity she could picture the time when she herself had slept in small beds like this one. For the first time, however, she marvelled at the long path she had travelled; it had seemed so brief because of its gentle monotony, its ease. And yet she was about to come into her prime . . . She laid her head down on the pillow next to Francette, her short curls mingling with the child's tangled shock of hair. Closing her eyes, she began to remember . . . Her childhood, full of bright days, happy holidays, petty, childish sorrows which somehow, Lord knows why, with the passing years become more precious than the joyous memories . . . Then her adolescence, in the dark shadow of the Great War, her engagement, a proper, dutiful French marriage of convenience, then motherhood – a good, happy life, well ordered, of course . . . And yet, tonight, she felt dissatisfied, disappointed, as if she could feel her poor heart was burning . . .

She got up, walked over to the window and stepped out on to the narrow wooden balcony planted with flowers; they smelled pungent and fresh. The summer night glistened . . . The empty little beach carved out by the sea was down below, the beach where Yves had waited for her, called out to her . . . That brief, magical moment had such a dreamlike quality about it that she now wondered if it had actually happened; a distinct feeling of unreality had stayed with her. But then, little by little, that changed . . . The longer she stood there, in the dark perfumed night, the more the present moment became blurred, vague, as if it were a dream, while the memory of that other moment grew stronger, more momentous, flowing through her heart and body in waves. Instinctively she reached out as if she were trying to sculpt the face she had caressed, the outline of the body she had held close; she looked as if she were carving the empty air, feeling her way, but confidently, as if she were a blind artist. Then, suddenly, she started shaking all over: beneath her fingers she thought she could feel the shape of his full, delicate mouth. She clenched her teeth: what she was feeling was akin to terror, yet it felt at the same time so painful and so wonderful that she whispered out loud, as if she were calling the name of a passer-by: 'Love?'

Later on, in the room next door to Francette's, when

Denise climbed back into the bed where her husband had slept, and when she instinctively reached out for the familiar shape of his large body under the sheets, Denise finally thought of him: her trusting, affectionate companion. She felt such pity for him that her eyes filled with tears; she was very fond of him. When he was with her she was bored and was content to think of other things, yet she did everything in her power to make life pleasant for him, to respond to his love with a great deal of affection and sensitive understanding. But when all was said and done she had deceived him. She made no excuses for herself. She knew very well that she had cheated him. Love . . . or rather, a brief romantic adventure: she would give her heart, of course, but he, the man, would only be interested in satisfying his vanity or his desire. She wanted nothing to do with the superficial poetry of some romantic novel. She understood only too well . . . Like all men, he would woo her the whole day long and then, in the evening, he would knock at her door, and it would last for three weeks, or a bit longer, or a bit less, and then they would separate, as if they were strangers. She wanted no part of it. She could picture the electric look in Yves's eyes when she saw him the next day, an expression she was familiar with because she had seen it more than once in the eyes of men who had found her attractive. Until today, she'd just laughed, but . . . now . . . She began to cry, her heart full of immense, vague, tender pity, pity for herself, for her husband, abroad all alone – he might even be ill – but most especially pity for Yves, for the likely suffering his unrequited love might bring him.

She decided that when she saw him the next day she would

be cold and distant. But all morning long he played with Francette on the beach. He barely looked up when he spoke to her; he seemed more embarrassed than she was, which melted her resolve. That evening, when he asked if she wanted to go for a walk before dinner, she went, her heart pounding, but determined to resist his inevitable words of love. But he said nothing. The sun was setting over the sea amid swirling storm clouds. It was high tide; waves rolled and crashed, white and grey, against the sea wall; the birds circled above with plaintive cries. He spoke to her of insignificant things, as he had before. They were sitting on the parapet; night was coming quickly; large drops of rain began to fall; he took her arm to help her run towards the hotel. For a moment she thought he was trembling a little, but he quickly regained his composure. The rain tumbled down in angry torrents; a sharp wind rose up, bending the tamarisk trees, crushing their flowers; Yves threw his jacket over Denise's shoulders; they ran like mad creatures through the rainstorm; he held her close to him; she could feel his taut fingers gripping her round the waist, but he remained obstinately silent, clenched his teeth, did not glance at her, while she surreptitiously raised fearful, yielding eyes to look at him.

8

The days passed and still he said nothing to her. He didn't try to kiss her; he didn't even allow himself to hold her cold, trembling hands longer than he should. He was too happy; with a kind of superstitious terror, he feared words as if they were a curse. He delighted in this moment in his life as if it were a luxury; it was a beautiful, unexpected gift offered to him by fate: peace, time to himself, the sea, this enchanting woman. For the moment, simply being with her was all he needed. Instead of weighing heavily, his long period of abstinence was something precious to savour, as if he had rediscovered his childhood. His desire for her caused him the kind of exquisite pain that is a pleasure to prolong, like when you are thirsty, at the height of summer, and you hold an ice-cold glass, misted with cool beads of water, to your lips for a long time, without drinking from it. He had experienced enough of life to understand the importance of his exhilaration and he jealously nurtured his emotion with pride, as if it were a rare flower. It was strange, but he had the impression of absolute security with her . . . the way men looked at her – in the morning on the beach, or in the evening when she came down into the hotel wearing a low-cut dress and diamond necklace – left him with a profound sense of calm: he was sure of her; he knew she was his, docile, at peace because of his feigned indifference, yet more intimately bound to him by everything that remained unexpressed between them than by the most passionate declarations of love. He was waiting, not out of any conscious ulterior motive, but because of a kind of innate indolence that was now more powerful than gestures or words.

But summer was nearly over; the weather was changing; the holiday villas closed up, one after the other. In the morning, the long beach was utterly deserted under a pale sky clouded by sudden showers. Instead of taking long siestas on the warm sand, they went for walks. With Yves, Denise walked through the Basque country, down little winding lanes along the Pyrenees, through forests, turning gold at the start of autumn, past sleepy villages where night fell more quickly than elsewhere because the high mountains plunged them in shadow at sunset. One day, as happy as a child, he picked some blackberries for Francette in a little forest at the edge of the Nivelle river while she ran her bare hands and arms through the water; at every moment they had the magical sense of growing younger, of returning to a kind of forgotten innocence.

There were still a few beautiful days towards the end of September. Yves suggested to Denise that they go to see the celebration in Fuenterrabia: it was an ancient ceremony enjoyed as much by the French as by the Spanish. In Fuenterrabia they fired cannon and rifle shots; there was music and noise and dust; groups of children with berets pulled down over one ear held each other round the waist, blocked the narrow lanes, shouted and sang at the top of their lungs; men on horseback galloped in from all directions at a furious pace; their horses whinnied, frightened by the din and the smell of gunpowder; carts drawn by mules decked out in pompoms and little bells wobbled along the sharp paving stones, rearing up when the enormous cars drove by; all of Biarritz, Saint Sebastian and the Spanish provinces was there, from Irun to Pamplona. Dirty-faced brats were fighting, shouting incomprehensible insults at each other in a cross between Basque and Castilian; beautiful young girls with flowing hair walked by wearing embroidered shawls; the ones from the furthest provinces wore chignons high on their heads and combs decorated with flowers; some of the older women still wore black mantillas. Everyone was laughing, shouting, singing, bickering, bumping into each other round the fountain and outdoor stalls where they sold lemonade, fruit drinks, oranges, floury round cakes, rattles, balloons and fans. A wave of people blocked the narrow street. Denise had fun looking at the shops with their displays of rosary beads, crucifixes and Saints' medals. The very old houses had overhanging roofs that almost touched above the road; balconies were decorated with shawls, embroidered blankets, lace tablecloths. A swift peal of bells rang out from the old dark gilt church. Yves seated Denise in a small café and bought her some hot chocolate with cinnamon and a sherry; she didn't like the chocolate: it was too thick and sweet but she drank two or three glasses of the sherry, which was excellent. Her cheeks were hot and her eyes shone. She took off her hat and the sun through her curls made them look light and bluish, like smoke rings. They leaned over the railing to watch the procession go by; it was endless, with flags, rusty old cannons, drunken men who held on to their rifles with trembling hands. Then came the priests in their embroidered chasubles, raising a large image of the Virgin Mary, surrounded by lit candles. The crowd kneeled as they passed by and in the sudden silence the bells rang out even more wildly, making everything shake, or so it seemed, right down to the dark, ancient walls.

Everyone walked to the church; little by little the square began to empty; soon, only Denise and Yves remained on the balcony, along with a group of Spanish peasants who were drinking in a corner of the café. It was nearly dusk, the sky was pink and the mountains seemed closer, full of mysterious, cool shadows. Denise was silent, quite tipsy, her eyes staring intently at the brilliant diamond on her finger. The evening breeze ruffled her hair.

'My husband is coming back any day now,' she suddenly said.

Then, immediately embarrassed, upset, ashamed of her lie, she blushed. But he didn't notice.

'Soon?' he asked anxiously.

She made a vague gesture to avoid answering. She noticed, with a rush of emotion, that Yves's lips were trembling slightly.

'Will he come to collect you?' he murmured. Then he immediately added, almost to himself, 'It's over . . . this wonderful holiday is over . . . I'd forgotten . . . The first of October is in two days . . . In two days I'll be in Paris.'

'In two days,' she cried out.

He felt as if his heart had stopped beating. And she thought she must be going mad: had it been a month since she looked at a calendar? Hadn't she realised that autumn was coming? But then, really, what could it matter to her if he left, this stranger, this man she didn't really know?

'Denise,' he called out softly.

She didn't dare reply; she could barely breathe. He took her hand and placed it on his warm brow.

'Denise,' he simply murmured again.

Then she could hear his voice choked with emotion: 'I can't leave you. I can't live without you now.'

Then, forgetting she should say no, resist, make him desire her, she couldn't hold back the great tears that rolled down her cheeks.

'Neither can I,' she said, 'I can't live without you.'

9

That evening she waited for him. She didn't switch on the light; she sat on the bed, her hands folded between her knees. He had begged her to have dinner with him in Fuenterrabia or in one of those little inns with whitewashed walls nestled in the side of the mountains that, at night, look as isolated as a bandit's hideout. But they have wonderful Spanish wine, grapes, cool, clean rooms with beds surrounded by mosquito nets and wooden floors warmed by the sun during the day that felt good on your bare feet. She had refused because of Francette, so he had immediately agreed to take her back to Hendaye, without even a hint of resentment.

Oh, their return in a small boat on the Bidassoa river that reflected the shimmering pink of the evening sky . . . The weather-beaten old sailor with a gold earring in his left ear pretended to be asleep at the oars; the wind carried the taste and scent of salt. When they arrived in Hendaye it was already dark and enormous stars lit up the night. They hadn't noticed darkness fall: their lips touching, eyes shut, they held each other close as the boat glided gently, silently, over the black water . . .

Denise put her head between her trembling hands. In the next room a little voice called out: 'Mama.' Reluctantly, Denise stood up and went to her daughter. Francette was not asleep; her eyes were shining and she stretched out her arms towards her mother.

'Mummy, did you bring anything back for me?'

Denise always brought some little trinket back for her daughter, whether she went out for the day or to a ball; but today she had forgotten. Embarrassed for a moment, she quickly recovered. 'Of course,' she said confidently, 'I brought you back the smell of the fair. I nearly lost it on the way home but I didn't, it's still here. Can you smell it?'

Looking serious, she leaned in and offered Francette her cheek to sniff.

Francette breathed in as deeply as she could, convinced by her mother's earnest manner. 'It smells really good,' she said.

Then she asked: 'Mummy, when I'm a big girl, will I be able to go to the fair too?'

'Of course, my treasure.'

Then she asked: 'Will I be a big girl soon? Will I?'

'Very soon, if you're a good girl.'

Denise was touched and kissed the trusting little hand that was holding on to one of her fingers. She was happy that she felt neither the shame nor the remorse she had feared when looking at this innocent creature who fell so soundly asleep. Of course Francette would be a big girl very 'soon'. She too would wait at night for her Master.

If she'd had a son, Denise might have been more upset and ashamed. But standing before this future young woman whose lips would one day be sweet and covered in kisses, whose body would be eager for love, she could not understand the extent of her fall from grace. She kissed her, tucked her in, pulled the cover up to her chin and went out, quietly closing the door.

She sat down once more on the unmade bed in her room and waited, head bent, hands clenched, submissive, waiting for the sound of a man's imperious footsteps.

10

He had left her at dawn. She was sleeping, with her head buried in the crook of her arm. He almost had the impression that he had taken a young girl: she was so awkward, inexperienced and had such a delightful way of overcoming her modesty as she gave herself to him that it was almost as if she were a virgin. He had quickly realised that in spite of marriage and motherhood, she was not yet truly a woman.

Soon afterwards she was taking her time to get washed and dressed, when a telegram was slipped under her door. She grabbed it, opened it:

Arriving Hendaye 3 October. In good health. Kisses.

JACQUES

She lowered her head with a little – but oh so little! – remorse. Then she immediately began to think, to work out the dates . . . Yves would delay his departure for two days. She would make her husband go back to Paris with her right away; in any case, it was getting colder and Francette was becoming restless because she'd been at the seaside for so long. She would be in Paris on the 4th, the 5th at the latest. Her whole life would change: how happy she was going to be! Gone would be the long days when she gradually killed time with dress fittings and social calls; gone those interminable hours with nothing to do, gone the feeling of emptiness and boredom that poisoned her life and prevented her from being happy. They'd have to find a little hideaway; she knew that Yves had a bachelor flat, but it would be so much more fun to have two beautiful rooms that she would keep filled with flowers and where they would choose all the knick-knacks . . . And they could go on long walks through Paris! She knew he loved old streets and houses as much as she did; she imagined how good it would feel to wander the riverbanks in the evening, at dusk, when the little lanterns on the barges along the Seine lit up, filling the deserted quays with shadows. With joy she remembered certain little bistros along the still river that she had looked at with curiosity when coming home from visiting someone on the left bank. No one would find them there; they would buy roasted chestnuts from the man at the corner; they would browse in antique shops and find silly souvenirs – expensive and charming – for *their* hideaway, and books – they both loved very old bound books with yellowing pages and tiny worm holes. Sometimes he would take her to the countryside to the silvery woods in Fontainebleau, and when spring came, she would arrange to have dinner with him outside the city, under an arbour of flowers beside a pond with croaking frogs. For the idea never even crossed her mind that their love might end before spring returned: she was the kind of woman who can only imagine love as eternal. She had given herself to him passionately, completely, with the naïve, boundless confidence of the innocent child she still was, so she naturally expected that he too would give himself entirely to her. She crushed her husband's telegram, threw it on to the table without another thought and finished getting dressed. A sweet, powerful emotion filled her heart, the profound conviction that she had performed a rite that bound her to Yves for ever, something, in a word, that was akin to the adoring devotion of a wife.

The day passed strangely quickly; wind, rain and sudden flashes of lightning made the sea flare up like an immense expanse of silver. Without giving a thought to the mud that covered the paths, Denise and Yves walked through the countryside for one last time. Whipped by the storm, leaves were falling from the trees; in this region, where the weather can change incredibly swiftly, one rainy night had managed to transform the sunny landscape of the previous day into a desolate, autumnal scene. Teams of livestock passed by. Great birds followed each other inland from the sea, almost skimming the ground with the sound of swishing wings. Yves and Denise walked down to the old port; its rosy stone steps, polished for so many years by the sea, were as smooth and shiny as marble; reflected in the shimmering water were the ancient ramparts of the city, the small boats, Pierre Loti's little villa with its overgrown garden and faded green shutters. Yves held Denise close; his face – normally weary and somewhat sad – seemed young again with an expression of passionate tenderness.

It was then that Denise asked him to stay in Hendaye with her for two more days; her voice held a tone of certainty: she was totally confident of his reply. But to her great astonishment he immediately looked worried.

'But Denise,' he said, surprised, 'the day after tomorrow is the 1st of October . . . My holiday finishes then . . . In two days I have to be in Paris . . .'

'Is someone expecting you back?'

'My office is expecting me, unfortunately!'

'Oh, two days more, two days less, what difference would that make?'

'The difference would be that I'd lose my job,' he explained quietly.

She said nothing, at a loss for words. She had never thought of asking him what he did. Her husband had told her that Yves was rich; she vaguely thought he had something to do with business, like her husband and all the other men in her social circle, business that women know nothing about unless it is translated into actual sums, most often in the millions. She'd been spoiled as a girl, the only child of a wealthy industrialist, then a young wife doted upon by a husband who earned a lot of money, so certain aspects of the material world, not surprisingly, were unknown to her. She realised that Yves was nothing more than an employee, and the idea of him being a lowly office worker who needed to earn a living shocked and upset her. Did that mean he was poor? But then, how could he afford to stay in Hendaye where he had to be spending at least a hundred francs a day? She didn't really understand . . . It is true that sacrificing necessities in order to have certain luxuries was a way of life that would have surprised many people. But when she saw the hardened look that suddenly appeared on the face of her lover, she realised she mustn't press him further. He was sitting on the steps by the port. She put her hand up to his face. Gently she lowered his unwilling head until it leaned submissively against her body, then she pressed it against her.

'Yves!' she said, then whispered, 'You'll go when you must . . . We still have a whole day together, my love . . .'

'Not really, Denise . . . I'm leaving at seven o'clock in the morning.'

'Ah, now you're really acting like a madman,' she cried out, laughing. 'Good Lord, why wear yourself out for no reason when there's an excellent train at seven in the evening that will get you to Paris the day after tomorrow in time to go to your office?'

'Because it only has sleeping cars and I'm travelling second class. I've lived the high life here on holiday and now I have to be careful how much I spend . . . It's not my fault, Denise, if I'm part of the new poor generation . . .' he added, with a kind of awkward pride. 'You mustn't hold it against me . . .'

'Oh, Yves,' she said.

Then she shyly added: 'I think you're even more precious to me, now that I know you're not happy . . .'

He smiled. 'I'm very happy, Denise; but never take my happiness away, my darling, because now, if you left me,

I don't think I'd be able to live all alone, the way I did before.'

Then he smiled the sweet smile that softened his harsh features and said once more: 'I'm very happy.'

He pressed his lips against her delicate hand and held it in his for a long time. 'When will you be back home, Denise?'

'On the 5th or 6th . . .'

'So late?'

'We're driving back,' she explained and suddenly felt somewhat embarrassed that she had such wealth, such luxuries, like the beautiful Hispano-Suiza that would get them back to Paris while Yves was buffeted about in a second-class train compartment.

But all he said was: 'It's a beautiful drive . . . I often did it when I was young . . . But the roads are bad, especially until you get to Bordeaux . . . be careful . . . Don't go too fast . . . I'll be terribly worried . . .'

11

Paris: the trees shed their yellow leaves that lay rotting in the thick mud on the pavements. The pace of life and the noise were incredible: the Automobile Show attracted the entire country to the capital, as it did each autumn.

Every year – true little Parisian that she was – Denise rediscovered the city with profound, sweet, somewhat silly emotion: the light fog, the smell of petrol and electricity, the misty sky coloured an 'elegant' grey above the tall houses, the hustle and bustle of the streets, and towards evening, the flood of lights rushing along the Champs Élysées to the Arc de Triomphe. Normally, as soon as she arrived, she would have a bath, give instructions to the servants, then go out for a long walk. She would return with rosy cheeks from being outdoors, and carrying armfuls of flowers – chrysanthemums and brightly coloured dahlias tinged with the scent of mushrooms and earth. Then she would organise the apartment, put the flowers in the vases, move all the knick-knacks, paintings and cushions around until she had returned the former warmth and familiar charm to the house that, abandoned for three months, felt impersonal and cold.

This year her pleasure at seeing Paris again had something intensely painful about it, something akin to sensuality. She had nearly cried out with joy on seeing Neuilly, and when the Arc de Triomphe appeared on the horizon her eyes had filled with tears. But when she got home, she didn't even glance at the apartment. She had her bath, slipped on a dressing gown, refused to put on the day outfit her chambermaid laid out for her and went into the little sitting room, her eyes staring at the clock, waiting for her husband to leave, which he did quite soon after. Then she had the telephone brought in to her, carefully closed the door and asked for the number of Yves's office, her voice trembling slightly.

'Hello,' replied a weary voice.

'Hello, Yves; it's me, Denise . . .'

A brief silence.

'Darling . . .' he said, but his tone of voice had barely changed. 'Did you have a good trip?'

She could sense there was someone standing near him. She quickly said a few banal things, then anxiously asked: 'I'll see you today, won't I?'

'Of course. I'd be delighted . . . I'm free after six-thirty.'

'Not before then?'

'Absolutely impossible.'

She knew very well that he had no choice but to speak the way he did: he was not alone; she could hear the murmur of conversations in the background. Nevertheless, such coldness coming from Yves chilled her, hurt her.

'Well, then, six-thirty,' she agreed. 'Do you want to meet near your office?'

'Yes.'

Then he quickly added in a low voice: 'Square de l'Opéra. There's a quiet little bar where no one ever goes. They have excellent port. It's just opposite my office. Shall we meet there?'

'Of course.'

'Good. See you there.'

Then she heard the brief click that ended their conversation. She slowly replaced the receiver, her heart suddenly heavy with an inexplicable feeling of disappointment and unease. Did he love her? Her hope was so intense that she wanted to see it as a certainty. And besides, she loved him so much, so very much . . .

It was four o'clock. She took her time getting dressed, carefully, with fresh attention to detail and a new way of intently studying her face and body in the mirror that alone was enough to give away that she was in love. But she was still ready early. She picked up a book, leafed through it without reading it and tossed it aside. Then she started to smooth out her unruly curls and changed her hat. Finally, at six o'clock, she went out.

She arrived at their meeting place just after six-thirty because there was a lot of traffic in Paris; but Yves wasn't there yet. She sat down at a small table hidden away in a corner. It was an English bar, tiny, sparkling clean, with a serious, 'respectable' look about it. It was almost empty; one couple sat at a nearby table smoking and staring into each other's eyes in silence.

Denise ordered a glass of port and waited. She felt embarrassed, nervous; she blushed intensely when the barman brought her some magazines. When he glanced discreetly at her, he looked blasé but a little sorry for her, as if he were thinking: 'Not another one.'

Finally Yves appeared. She felt as if her heart might leap out of her chest.

'Are you well?' she whispered in a quiet, toneless voice.

'Denise,' was all he said. But he looked overcome with emotion; he kissed her hand passionately. 'At last you're here with me.'

She smiled.

'Are you happy to see me? You sounded so cold earlier on the telephone.'

'What?' he asked, surprised. 'Didn't you realise there were people all around me?'

'Yes, but . . .'

He had sat down; he began asking her questions about her trip, how she was, with an intense look of tenderness and happiness in his eyes. But she glanced at him furtively, sadly; he seemed weary, older, with dark circles under his eyes and a bitter expression round his mouth. Something indefinable was missing: that air of youthfulness, of elegance that men lose as soon as they can no longer take trouble over their appearance. She recalled how impeccable he had looked when he came down to dinner in Hendaye after bathing and shaving: like a young Englishman in his evening suit, his dinner jacket showing off his attractive body.

'Do you want to come back to my apartment?' he asked.

'I'd like to very much but I have to be home at seven o'clock . . . My husband is always home by then . . .'

'Ah! Never mind then,' he said, annoyed.

'Does your office close so late every day, Yves?' she asked.

He made a weary gesture. 'Oh, I'll work something out . . . but it will be difficult . . .'

Then, with a kind of forced cheerfulness, he added: 'I'm free tomorrow, Denise, completely free . . . It's Saturday and I only work a five-day week . . . You'll come and see me, won't you, my darling?'

'Oh, how could you doubt it? Of course I will . . .'

It was five to seven. Yves hailed a taxi. Inside the cab he grabbed Denise and crushed her in his arms. 'My darling, my love . . .'

She melted into his arms, very pale, her eyes closed. He bruised her cheeks, her neck, the delicate skin on her wrists with passionate kisses. Then he had the driver stop outside a florist's shop and got out; she waited a moment for him. He came back carrying a single orchid, wrapped in tissue paper, as if it were a jewel, an expensive thing of beauty with twisted petals and a velvety trumpet of deep red, glowing with fire.

'Oh! It's so beautiful!' cried Denise, enthralled.

'Do you really like it?' asked Yves. 'I like orchids though I prefer roses. But they didn't have any left, so I got this. There are women who look like these flowers, aren't there?' he added, smiling. 'At least, that's what they think. Not you, fortunately. You're so pure and simple. You're like a rose, Denise, really you are. You are like one of those fragrant roses that grow in English gardens, with delicate, flesh-pink petals and a deeper colour at the heart; and their scent reminds me of your perfume, my darling, it truly does.'

Denise had buried her head in the hollow of Yves's shoulder and was listening to him speak, overwhelmed, her eyes closed, drinking in his words, like a child hearing a fairy tale. He fell silent and began rocking her very gently. Then she whispered 'I love you', offering her passionate heart to him. All her feminine instinct made her expect to hear him say the same words back to her, the eternal 'I love you', like an echo, sensed even more than heard. But he said nothing. He just pressed her more tightly to him.

12

She was rather apprehensive about going to his apartment: she was afraid he might live in some nondescript furnished place where she would feel ill at ease. She was pleasantly surprised when she went into the apartment; he had managed to hold on to it since 1912. You could tell that every object had been chosen with love; it had comfortable furniture, bought in England before the war, and a large fireplace where logs were burning brightly. A little table was set up in the bedroom; there was some fruit in a splendid Bohemian crystal bowl and wine in a small old silver decanter; everything was lit by a pair of lamps with rose-coloured shades mounted on two old silver-gilt candelabra of meticulous workmanship.

Yves seemed truly at home among all these beautiful, expensive objects; how surprising it was to see the sudden change in his face, she thought to herself. Yesterday he was old, lifeless, almost ugly; today he was young and handsome.

She met Pierrot, the white Spitz who looked like a curly sheep out of some pastoral scene, with a pale pink ribbon round his neck. Then he showed her his favourite but modest collection of perfume flasks. He insisted she accept one as a gift; it dated back to Elizabeth I of England and bore the princess's coat of arms carved in darkened silver on deep blue glass that shone beneath the light like a precious stone.

'Please, please take it,' he urged, when she first tried to refuse. 'If you only knew what a rare pleasure it is for me to give presents, too rare, sadly . . . Please . . .'

Then he showed her portraits of his family; he told her about his father and some of his romantic adventures, especially the time when he fell in love with a Russian artist and left his wife and son to be with her; he'd lived with her near Nice for almost a year, in a villa called 'Sniegurochka', 'snow maiden'. Since she was very blonde and adored white, all the rooms in the house were white, decorated with marble, alabaster, crystal, and white peacocks roamed the grounds were planted exclusively with white flowers – tuberoses, camellias, snow-white roses – while wonderful swans glided across its three lakes. She had died there, so he went back to his wife.

'She forgave him, as she had so many other times,' Yves said. 'She always forgave him . . . his betrayals were like works of art . . . You couldn't hold it against him . . . he was irresistible . . . He had the hypnotic charm of people who are loved too much. It's true that when he was in love he gave himself entirely, and each time, for ever . . . We don't know how to love like that any more . . .'

He was sitting at Denise's feet, leaning against her legs, in front of the fireplace; he stared into the fire.

'Why?' asked Denise.

He made a vague gesture.

'Ah, why? I don't know . . . First of all, life these days is too harsh . . . The effort we used to spend on passion, on love, is now used up on the thousand stupid, poisonous little problems we face every day . . . To love the way they did, you have to be wealthy and have all the time in the world . . . and of course, they were so happy . . . their lives were peaceful, secure, easy, pleasurable . . . they needed emotions, but all we need is rest. And besides, in the end, perhaps love demands marble palaces, white peacocks and swans – more than we like to admit.'

She leaned down towards him and put her hands on his shoulders. 'Yves, do you love me?' she asked and her voice did not sound like a woman in love murmuring 'Do you love me?' as if it were an affirmation, divinely certain in advance of the response. Quite the opposite: her voice was full of anxiety and suffering. All the same, she hoped. He remained silent.

'What good are words, Denise?' he finally said. 'Words mean nothing.'

'Say it to me anyway, please . . . I need to know.'

'It's just . . . I wonder if I'm capable of loving, loving the way I want to.' He sighed. 'And yet, Denise, I feel you're so very, very precious to me. The desire I feel for you is filled with immense tenderness . . .'

'That's what love is,' she stammered, staring at him, imploring him, her heart nearly breaking.

But all he said was, 'If you think that's what love is, Denise, then I love you.'

For the first time she felt a kind of barrier rise up between their two hearts, like a border crossing that was not well marked out but was impossible to breach. She said nothing; she preferred to close her eyes, to forget about herself, not to see, not to be reassured, not to lose him, especially not to lose him. And as he kissed her she furtively wiped away two large tears that welled up and overflowed from her heavy heart.

13

One Sunday in December, Denise's mother, Madame Franchevielle, came to lunch at the Jessaints' along with her cousin, Jean-Paul. He was a good-looking young man of twenty-three, with bold eyes and the pouting red lips of a pageboy. It was a beautiful winter's day: freezing cold, clear, with bright sunshine. A pinkish light lit up the dining room so the reflections from the crystal danced over the walls. Denise's face was suddenly clearly seen in the brightness: it was pale, drawn, with the hint of the creeping shadows you sometimes see on young faces, outlining the eyelids, the corners of their mouths, places where future wrinkles will appear, almost like a subtle warning.

'Are you ill, Denise?' asked Madame Franchevielle.

At the age of forty-nine, Denise's mother was still an exquisite woman who had no qualms about going to a ball with her daughter in the evening wearing a sleeveless gown, her arms bare despite the cruel light of the chandeliers. Even today, in the pitiless bright sunshine, she looked younger than Denise. She was expertly made-up, with beautiful gleaming teeth and luxurious, shiny hair; she looked healthy and was always in good spirits. Denise loved her a great deal; she was grateful to her for having been a good mother: attentive, intelligent and, hiding her intense affection beneath a somewhat distant, mocking exterior. She had not been very outgoing or demonstrative, but Denise had a clear memory from long ago of the nine nights when she had scarlet fever: through her high fever and delirium, she could see her mother's eyes looking into hers, fixed to hers, with a stubborn expression that willed her to recover, a determination that had, in fact, kept her from dying. Because she was so attractive and had been widowed so young, Madame Franchevielle had had, and undoubtedly still had, discreet, tasteful affairs. Denise was vaguely aware of them but did not wish to know any details, and these affairs – rather than diminishing her mother in her eyes – almost increased Denise's respect for her, for they made her mother the symbol of the perfect woman, someone who misses nothing, sees everything and understands even more. Madame Franchevielle's insight was renowned; her daughter had never managed to hide anything from her. And even today, when her mother questioned her, she felt uncomfortable and blushed without replying.

'I hope you're not going to make me a grandmother again!' cried Madame Franchevielle with horror, pretending not to understand.

'No, no, don't worry, Mama,' said Denise with a sad little smile, so Madame Franchevielle immediately and adroitly changed the subject.

As the coffee was about to be served, the guests went

from the dining room through to the cosy sitting room and library next door; it was full of pretty prints, flowers and rare books. Jean-Paul stood up to help Denise.

'That's it, you can play at being hostess,' Denise said to him, with the same tight crease around her lips that she hoped would pass for a smile.

'Now I'm sure of it,' said Jean-Paul as he skilfully handed out the cups.

'Sure about what?'

'You have a lover, my pretty . . . Poor Jacques, he's . . .'

Jean-Paul made a mischievous gesture behind Jessaint's back. Denise turned pale.

'All right, all right, don't get into a state . . . But you do look awful, Denise. Aren't you feeling well, or is it love that's putting such a strain on you?'

'Be quiet, I'm begging you, just be quiet!' she said again.

There was such weariness in her eyes that Jean-Paul looked at her with an expression of sincere, affectionate sympathy.

'Poor little Denise . . . You're suffering . . . Ah, since you had to go and make a cuckold of your fat, jovial husband, why didn't you hear me out when I was here last year?'

She couldn't help but smile as she recalled the moment when Jean-Paul had declared his feelings for her with adolescent enthusiasm, half mockingly, half passionately; he had ended up chasing her round the tables and from corner to corner with such zeal that his aggression soon turned into a kind of game, just like the blind man's bluff they used to play as children.

'My poor Jaja,' she said, calling him by the nickname she gave him as a child, 'hear you out? You were as coarse and naïve as a young cockerel.'

'That's how it looked to you because I didn't swear eternal love or bring the moon and the stars into how I felt. Denise, my girl, you're the last of the romantics. Words will be the death of you. But words mean nothing.'

'You think that as well, do you?' she asked, surprised. 'But you're still young. Were you in love with me?'

'I wanted you, of course, and I always had a soft spot for you in my heart, but I don't know if that's love,' he answered honestly.

'You're all the same,' she murmured, her voice breaking a little . . . 'affection, desire . . . a soft spot . . . Why not just admit it's love? Are you afraid of the word?'

'And of the thing itself, Denise . . . And besides, ever since the war, who knows what love is any more . . . Listen, when I was chasing after you, I adored you, as you would call it. And then, when you sent me packing, I cried like a baby, you know, and yet, the entire time, I felt that I'd get over it, because in the end, there's no woman alive you can't get over . . . We men know that from birth.'

'Well, we women don't know it.'

'You and the other delicate souls destined to suffer. You treat us like boors because you offer us eternity on a silver platter and we have the impertinence to turn it down. But you're the exceptions. Long ago, other women put into practice a variation on Baudelaire's line: "Be charming, be silent, and get the h**l out."'

Fiddling with the spoons, he purposely brushed his hand against Denise's.

'Still, if you ever need someone to help you pass "those long twilight hours . . ." – that's what they're called, aren't they? – then think of Jaja . . . But let's change the subject. Now, I'm no longer speaking to Denise but to Madame Jessaint, wife of the super-rich Jessaint (Jacques) . . . remember – oh, Denise – how we played together, how I helped you steal jam, how I was best man the day of your solemn marriage, when . . .'

'So you need money?'

'I can't hide anything from you.'

'Do you have a little girlfriend?'

'No, I have a little car . . . She's better than a woman but just as expensive, and Papa sent me packing when I tried to touch him for money last week.'

'You don't have a girlfriend?'

'I do, but she doesn't cost me anything; she's got an old man.'

'Oh, Jean-Paul!'

'What do you mean, oh, Jean-Paul! If I spend money, I get told off and if I save money I get told off.'

'Is she pretty?'

'Oh! Yes, she's dainty, she's dark, dazzling, with a rather long, slim bonnet . . .'

'A what?'

'A bonnet. Didn't you know that cars have bonnets?'

'You mean you're talking about your car?'

'Of course, what else would I be talking about?'

'Jean-Paul, you're just too charming . . . You can have two thousand francs. Now go and get us some liqueurs.'

He slipped out without even thanking her. Once she had her coffee, she curled up in her favourite place, on a cushion near the fireplace, and watched the dancing reddish flames.

Her mother's voice pulled her out of her daydream. 'Are you asleep, Denise? I left my hat in your room. Will you come with me?'

Once in Denise's bedroom, Madame Franchevielle walked over to her daughter and took her by the shoulders. 'My darling, you do look terribly sad . . . Tell your mama what's upsetting you so much.'

'I can't.'

'Is there anything I can do?'

'No, Mama, thank you . . . Don't worry . . . Everything's all right . . . Maybe if things get too painful to handle, maybe I'll tell you then . . . But don't ask me anything now.'

Madame Franchevielle squinted her pretty, short-sighted eyes that seemed to look straight into the heart, but all she said was, 'All right, my darling.'

By three o'clock Denise was alone. Madame Franchevielle had left; Jessaint also went out, telling her he had to call on some people.

'Now Jacques is becoming a socialite,' said Denise slightly ironically, with that hint of aggressive annoyance that women can't help feeling towards their husbands when their lovers make them unhappy.

But she was careful not to go with him or hold him back. Then she sent Jean-Paul away because he kept following her around.

A slim, diagonal ray of light the colour of ripe apricots slipped into the sitting room, lighting up the small ivory clock. Denise looked at the time. The day before, like every day when she said goodbye to Yves she had asked: 'Will I see you tomorrow?' Every day she promised herself that she would wait for him to be the first to ask the same question, but every day, at the last minute, she was the one who, shy and fearful, whispered it quickly and softly. Although, once or twice, she had had the courage to say nothing; the next day he had telephoned her at the normal time, but the insecurity she felt until then had nearly driven her mad. Insecurity . . . that was what really made her suffer. She was almost certain that he wasn't cheating on her. Why? He had neither the time, nor the opportunity, nor even the temptation, surely. 'But that, that's nothing,' she thought. 'That's forgivable.' What she needed, just as she needed air to breathe, was reassurance that she was loved. She didn't know it though. She didn't know anything. He was always weary, tired, distracted, annoyed, yet she could sense his tenderness and physical attraction for her. Nevertheless, she felt that she was the only one holding on to their love, holding on with all her might. If she left him, she knew he would not try to stop her because he was indolent and innately despondent, and so she felt an enormous moral weight, as if she had to carry a precious burden in her weak, trembling hands, a burden that was simply too heavy. And yet . . . he wasn't cruel; he was dignified and sensitive, but he didn't understand, he couldn't sense her suffering.

Whenever she asked 'Will I see you tomorrow?' he would

reply: 'I'll call you, my darling.' To him it was quite simple: she told him again and again that she was free, that she would organise her days around him; he was very busy at the office, with business and the thousand problems of a poor bachelor, which he didn't want to discuss with her. He believed it was better to arrange their meetings at the last minute than risk allowing some unexpected circumstance to prevent them from seeing each other. It was very logical, but waiting for the phone to ring was a daily agony, a slow, sophisticated torture that she couldn't explain but which he should have understood. And it was precisely his inability to understand that was one of the most terrible things she felt was lacking: the strange sensitivity that links two people, unites them into a single being, makes them enjoy the same pleasures and suffer the same pain. Yes, there was something missing between them, something elusive and vague, something, perhaps, that is quite simply known as reciprocal love.

Three o'clock . . . she still felt light-hearted, confident. It was always the same. She picked up a book and read a few pages with interest. By ten past three she was starting not to take in anything; words had lost all meaning; they were nothing more than black symbols against a white background that danced before her eyes; she read and reread the same sentences over and over again: 'The moon, high in the sky, resembled the tip of a cone of white light . . .' 'The moon, high in the sky . . .' 'The moon . . .' She didn't understand and snapped the book shut. She picked up a nail buffer and began obsessively polishing her nails, staring blankly at their shiny surface; but her spirit was too restless; she stood up and hesitated for a moment in the hallway. She really had no idea what to do. There was nothing she could do . . . nothing, nothing . . . She opened the nursery door. Francette was sitting in a high chair next to her English nanny, cutting out pictures. For a brief moment the cool calmness in this room imperceptibly filled Denise with a feeling of gentle peace. Francette chattered on in her high-pitched, birdlike voice; flames crackled in the fireplace, the black cat licked himself and purred like a kettle on the boil. She sat down next to her daughter and stroked her hair. Then, suddenly, she jumped up anxiously.

'Wasn't that the telephone?'

'No, Madame,' the Englishwoman calmly replied.

Nevertheless Denise was worried. She told herself that she might not be able to hear the shrill sound of the telephone from the nursery; it would be muffled by the heavy curtains, and the servants were so busy with other things. She couldn't stay where she was; every time a bus passed by in the street or Francette tapped the porcelain animals from Copenhagen that decorated her room, making them jingle, she would shudder and strain to listen. Suddenly she leaped up and practically ran back to her room: this time she was sure.

'Hello, hello . . .'

It was some acquaintance. She had to suffer her questions, pretend to be interested in boring banalities. Finally she put down the receiver; she was trembling all over . . . A quarter to four . . . Yves might have tried to telephone . . . Silently, she went and sat down on a low chair between the window and the fireplace. It was so quiet! In the empty apartment she could hear the slightest sound: the creaking of furniture, the muffled footsteps of a servant in the dining room; downstairs the heavy door to the street closed with the muted sound of a lid shutting . . . Outside a car passed by on the Avenue d'Iéna; it was Sunday and as quiet as a country lane . . . Then once again there was the crushing, deathly silence, the unique calm of a Sunday in the wealthy part of Paris.

Denise rested her elbows on her knees and held her head in her hands; she stared at the fire, her mind a blank, the way you sometimes do when trying to sleep and you force yourself to go numb, your mind empty, eyes staring out into space, trying not to think, my God, especially trying not to think! But gradually, slowly, almost against her will, she turned her face to the dark corner where the telephone stood. She seemed to be imploring that inanimate object, as if it were a little god made of wood and metal, ironic and silent. Past four o'clock . . . He wasn't going to call . . . He'd forgotten . . . No, it wasn't possible, he hadn't forgotten . . . But why wasn't he calling, my God? Why? Oh! The torment of sitting there, hands freezing cold, heart barely beating, life itself hanging in the balance, dependent on that horrible little telephone – so mocking, so silent – gleaming in its dark corner. The torture of waiting in silence for its crackling ring, in vain. Four-thirty . . . The clock chimed. She started out of her chair, her face white . . . Then she began to cry, quietly, in despair. Suddenly the phone rang, loudly, clearly, insolently.

She grabbed the receiver, willing her hand not to shake, wary that it might be someone else. But no, it was Yves; she heard his deep, rather husky voice.

'Denise?'

'Is that you, my darling?'

'Denise, I'm terribly busy . . . I could see you in about an hour, maybe an hour and a half. I'm sorry.'

'On Sunday?'

'I'm afraid so.'

She could hear a slight harshness in his voice. She weakened at once.

'Whenever you like. At your place?'

'No, not at my place.'

'Why not?'

'I'll explain everything to you.'

'Where then?'

'Are you alone?'

'Yes.'

'I'll call in at your house.'

'Fine,' she said coldly, disappointed, defiant.

But he had already hung up. Yet a great wave of relief spread through her. She suddenly remembered she had a thousand things to do; she hadn't checked the figures the butler had given her; she hadn't tried on the hat she'd had sent to her from Chez Georgette; she had to sort out some lace to put on the lingerie she'd ordered. She cheerfully attended to these various chores for about half an hour; then she went to fix her hair, put on some make-up, add more perfume to her neck and arms in the places he normally kissed; she put on his favourite dress, laid out the teacups on a table, poured some port into the small decanter that shone like a ruby, arranged the flowers, put some cigarettes in the black and green lacquer box from Moscow that he liked and set everything near the fireplace beneath the rosy glow of the lamp. And then, once more, she began to wait. Her entire life now consisted of waiting. Waiting for the phone to ring, waiting for his visit, waiting for their rendez- vous . . . Ah! Love meant such horrible suffering. But why? It wasn't the way they touched each other that bound her to him. Like most very young women, she was not sensual, and when she was in his arms she was not truly happy, always tormented by a vague sense of anguish that ate away at her, like some illness she could feel deep inside, but without knowing its name. In spite of her insecurity, however, some- times – oh, so rarely! – when she sat on his lap and slipped her hand through the fine silk shirt on to her lover's chest, to the place where she could feel his heart beating – some- times she felt filled with a divine sense of peace . . . And she was prepared to endure any amount of suffering for that rare moment of delightful, peaceful, love.

But for now she was still waiting . . . Her eyes were glazed, her nerves numb; only her sense of hearing was alive, marvel- lously sharpened, straining to hear the slightest sounds in the street . . . Footsteps getting closer, going past the house, fading in the distance . . . a car slowing down, stopping, no, driving away . . . Then the muted hum of the lift and the clear ringing of the doorbell on the floor above . . . Why was he so late? What if he'd been in an accident? Taxis crashed at the corner of her street every day . . . And why hadn't he wanted her to come to his apartment? Her imagi- nation exaggerated everything, monstrously magnified and distorted the slightest detail . . . Who knows? Perhaps he was cheating on her? How would she know? Perhaps he had another mistress? Perhaps he had grown tired of her and had gone back to a former lover? Or maybe he'd met someone new? She imagined her lover lying next to another woman, remarking in a bored tone of voice: 'Too bad; Denise will have to wait today . . .' She tortured herself endlessly with such thoughts, as if she were a sick child . . .

And then she felt another kind of terror, the terror that always lived deep in her heart, like the fear of death that slumbers in cowardly men and awakens at certain horrible moments to sneer at them: the fear that he would leave her . . . Oh! Not the melodramatic break-up scene, as it used to be called . . . That kind of scene doesn't happen any longer, not even in the theatre . . . Why such melodrama for something so insignificant? These days people just left: one fine day they simply didn't turn up for the rendezvous and it was over, they disappeared . . . It's what they called 'dropping a woman' and it's very decent, very practical, very kind . . .

Meanwhile the hands of the clock marked the passing minutes, urgently, rapidly, like insidious little insects that gnaw at you and file away carrying a tiny piece of your life.

Denise waited.

How did that poem by Maxim Gorky go?

> *To love without being loved,*
> *To lie in bed without sleeping,*
> *To wait when no one is coming,*
> *Three things that leave you dying.*

14

'And there you have it, my friend,' concluded Jean Vendômois, 'that's the life I lead . . . In northern Finland with no communication whatsoever with the outside world, at the edge of the Arctic Circle . . . It's the life of a pioneer in Canada a century ago. Nine months of the year, the kind of winter that's impossible to imagine until you've seen it . . . Snow . . . whiteness, a crystal-clear sky and the most wonderfully pure air . . . enormous deep forests slumbering beneath the snow . . . not a breath of wind, not a sound . . . just the sleigh bells . . . three months of summer when the sun never sets . . .'

'I see,' murmured Yves, his eyes wide in wonder.

They had been talking since lunchtime, forgetting even to drink the coffee set in front of them. Pierrot sat between their legs and raised his pointy pink nose towards them with the smiling expression such curly-haired dogs always have. Vendômois was a short, stocky man with intelligent eyes in a hardened, tanned, square face.

'. . . Just imagine it,' he said, leaning in towards Yves,

'imagine . . . far from Paris, far from the difficult, idiotic way of life we inherited after the war . . . Out there, you have absolute freedom . . . And the feeling that what you do with your own two hands is real work, that you're actually creating something . . . Listen, three years ago there were only twenty-two horses in my village; now there are a hundred and seventy-five . . . It's fantastic . . . Ah! My dream is to build a railway to link my village with Haparanda; at the moment we have no choice but to move our goods using horses and reindeer . . . A railway would mean earning a fortune, certain success, do you see?'

'Of course I see,' exclaimed Yves loudly to his friend, 'it's wonderful.'

'Yes, it is wonderful . . . Oh, Yves, come back with me . . . What are you going to do here? You'll stagnate, you'll get bogged down in some monotonous routine . . . Do you really think the restricted life of a petty employee in an office is for you? You'd be your own boss over there, Yves . . . And also, you know, this factory may be nothing at the moment, it's tiny, but it's growing, expanding . . . it's wonderful to watch it grow every year, like a child . . . Let me explain . . . we manufacture matches, as you know . . . well, those forests are inexhaustible and you can buy them from the government for almost nothing because they need foreign income; those forests can provide all the wood you need, even for the packing cases, you see?'

He rattled off figures and Yves listened, his eyes shining.

'Five years of hard work and you'll earn back the fortune you once had . . . I'm not exaggerating, you know.'

'I know.'

The two friends fell into a long silence.

'How I envy you!' Yves said at last.

'Well then, come . . .'

Yves shrugged his shoulders and didn't reply.

Jean Vendômois looked at him more closely. 'So there's a woman, is there?'

'Yes, a woman.'

'What do such trifling things matter?'

'She's the suffering type.'

'Really! You have to put us first.'

'I . . . I just can't.'

'So she's a pretty little creature, a plaything, then?'

'No, she's a real woman, devoted, sincere and loving . . . That's why I can't . . .'

'My poor boy, that's ridiculous . . .'

'I know it is.'

'Listen,' Vendômois continued, 'I'm going to sign a contract with an Englishman in an hour . . . But if you say "yes", I'll send him packing . . . Just give me your word and I'll go back there and wait for you . . .'

'I can't give you my word.'

'You won't come then?'

Yves looked at the fireplace and said nothing.

Vendômois stood up. 'Too bad,' he said with a small sigh. 'Then I'll say goodbye, my friend; look after yourself.'

They gave each other a hug. Yves was pale as a ghost.

Before leaving, Vendômois added: 'Listen, if one day things don't work out . . . you never know . . . promise me that you'll come . . .'

'I promise.'

'All right then . . . goodbye.'

Alone again, Yves went back to the fire, knelt down, leaned his head against Pierrot's and let out a deep sigh, the brief, painful sob of a man, but with no tears.

'My boy, my good little boy,' he whispered, his face buried in Pierrot's fluffy coat, 'Oh! How wonderful it would be . . . Just imagine: living free, surrounded by nature, in the snow, in enormous deep forests, hunting, working, a healthy sort of work that uses the body as well as the mind, freedom . . . I'd take you with me . . . Oh! Peaceful evenings in a house made of wood, silence, the moon above the snow, the stars that Jean described, larger and more brilliant than ours . . . Work that leaves my arms aching with exhaustion, but with a free, happy heart . . . What a dream, my good little boy!'

He noticed some small photographs on the carpet that Vendômois had shown him; he'd either forgotten them or left them there on purpose. He picked them up. He saw the plains, wooden huts, lightweight sleighs pulled by reindeer, pine forests, clear, round lakes reflecting the birch trees . . .

He looked at them for a long time, then threw them on to the fire.

'Denise, my darling Denise,' he sighed, 'you'll never know what I'm sacrificing for you.'

15

When Yves arrived at Denise's over an hour late, he found
her huddled in a corner by the window, sobbing. At first he
was frightened.

'My God, Denise, what's wrong? Has something happened?'

She gestured that it wasn't that, unable to speak. He
wanted to take her in his arms. But she pushed him away,
her arms tense and stiff with rage.

'. . . You're selfish, selfish . . . Here I am mad with worry,
imagining heavens knows what, something awful, an accident . . . But no, you walk in without even deigning to
apologise, without a word . . .'

'You've hardly given me time to say anything,' he pointed
out coldly, his eyes suddenly hardening.

'Be quiet, leave me alone, you're horrible, cowardly,
cruel . . . you have no right, do you hear? No right to make
me suffer like this . . .'

She could barely speak.

He took a step towards the door. 'Denise, I think you

may be going mad . . . I'll come back when you're not so upset. Goodbye.'

She let out a sound like a wounded animal in pain: 'Yves, Yves, don't leave me . . . don't go, Yves . . .'

She clutched at him madly with her trembling hands, hung on to his clothes, his arms, his neck; he grabbed her and held her so tightly against him that his embrace was more like an act of violence than a caress. Little by little she calmed down; the wild beating of her heart grew still; she raised her small sad face to him: it was covered in tears, contorted, deathly pale.

'Yves . . .'

Then quietly, shyly, she begged him: 'You forgive me, don't you?'

He gave a slight shrug and looked at her with a strange expression, a combination of pity, tenderness and scorn.

They sat down very close to one another on the divan, in a dimly lit corner; in the fireplace, reddish, silvery embers sent off sparks every now and then that burst into bright flames before quickly dying out.

Denise rested her head against Yves's chest and felt a wonderful sense of relief, the kind of relaxed, voluptuous languor that sets in after a woman has been crying hysterically. From time to time a sob shook her whole body before slowly subsiding, like a swell after a great storm; her heart, so heavy just a while ago, seemed lighter now, like a block of ice that has melted leaving a wispy coat of salty water that moistened the corners of her eyes.

Surreptitiously, she watched Yves.

He was silent, overwhelmed, grave.

'You must never, ever do that again, Denise, do you under-stand?' he said quietly.

Some of her former bitterness stirred in Denise's unhappy heart.

'Where were you before?' she asked in a tone of voice that was almost hateful. 'Why didn't you come sooner?'

'I was with a friend,' he replied, in a deliberately cold, detached tone of voice.

She didn't dare say 'I don't believe you', but he could not help noticing the bitter, hard pinching of her lips. He stiffened and moved imperceptibly away from her. A kind of muted hostility was rising up between them. She could sense it; she wanted to ward it off, like an evil spell, with kisses, caresses; but he sat there tense, his mouth closed, his hands motionless.

Then she whispered: 'Yves, do you love me? Tell me you love me . . . You mean so much to me. Say something, talk to me . . .'

He remained stubbornly silent. She had the impression of desperately throwing herself against a locked door, beating it in vain with her painful head, like a sad little bird in a room with no light; and still she said over and over again with the awkward, terrible obstinacy of a woman: 'Say some-thing, talk to me . . .'

Finally, he replied: 'I don't know what to say, Denise, my darling Denise; give me calm, peace, affection . . . I need to feel your hands on my face, on my heart; I need your sweet, youthful voice laughing beside me . . . But I can't, I don't know how to talk of love . . . Think of how many years I have been silent . . . Don't force me to tell beautiful lies . . . I don't want to . . . I'm tired . . . Give me peace . . . I need peace . . .'

'But I do need to hear all those things,' she said, incensed. 'I do need to be told I'm the most beautiful, the most precious and the only woman in your life. I need to hear those words, even if I know they are lies . . . I do . . .'

'I can't give you what you're asking of me. It's not my fault, Denise. Perhaps I'm as lacking in feelings as I am in money, I don't know . . . But I am giving you everything I am capable of giving . . .'

'That's not very much . . . and meanwhile, I'm suffering,' she said softly.

'Well,' he sighed, gently pushing her away, 'then let's end it.'

A sudden icy chill swept through her. 'Do you really mean that?'

'I don't want you to be unhappy.'

'Oh!' she said, 'I'd prefer a thousand times over to be unhappy because of you than to lose you, you know that very well . . .'

Silently, she placed her warm cheek next to his. 'You're selfish,' she whispered sadly, but with no anger.

'You're selfish,' he replied with a strange little weary sigh.

And they sat there without speaking, holding each other, he looking far off into the distance, she looking at him.

16

Yves opened his bedroom door and, before closing it again, he called out towards the dim recesses of the servant's pantry, as he did every evening: 'Run my bath, please, Jeanne,' he said, sounding exhausted, '. . . quickly . . .'

Then he dropped down into the nearest armchair.

He had a bath every evening because he didn't have time to take one before leaving for the office. At eight o'clock in the morning he had to make do with a hasty wash with cold water, shivering in the badly heated bathroom, while beyond the window the ugly grey light of day began to shroud the trees, the sky and the endless rooftops. After four years, Yves still could not get used to the shudder he felt when he woke up, the slight sickness and the nervous desire to yawn and stretch out: it reminded him of nights in the trenches when the alarm sounded, bringing him to his feet at dead of night, violently breaking into his dreams. For the rest of the day he felt a vague unease, exhaustion; he would long for the moment when he could relax and finally sink his weary body

into the deep bath, full of warm, scented water, just as young
boys who are confined in school all day imagine being at
home in the evening with the lamp lit, a steaming soup tureen
on the table, surrounded by their family. Along with the dust
accumulated during the day, he felt he was shedding his
tiredness, his bad mood, his worries and the whole physical
and mental atmosphere of the office he hated so much.

Today, in fact, his routine work seemed more especially
painful than usual: like a highly strung woman, he felt the
weather tyrannise him with its overwhelming power. It had
been drizzling since morning: a dull, light rain fell slowly,
splashing against the windows with a mean, insistent sound
that set your teeth on edge. And as soon as Yves looked
up, he saw the dark, muddy streets; sad people hunched
under glistening umbrellas, rushing about like a herd of
animals pursued by an invisible hunter; large neon signs
flashed in the darkened skies. Around five o'clock it stopped
raining; a ribbon of pink appeared on the horizon; for a
moment the damp streets reflected its light and shone like
amethysts; but when the green-shaded lamps in the office
were switched on, outside it was suddenly night. The click-
clack of typewriters, the smell of ink . . . sharp pains in
their hunched backs and necks, stinging eyes . . . columns
of figures in rows, getting longer and longer . . . a pile of
letters that never seemed to dwindle, like the sack of gold
belonging to the kobolds in German legend, the sack you
were condemned to empty and refill endlessly, for a thousand years, then another thousand years, for having caught
the ancient Rhine playing with the golden sparkles on the
waves at sunset . . . these faces around him, always the

same, conscientious employees bent over their work . . .
he simply couldn't understand how his job, that for his
subordinate would have been a dream come true – a desk
near the window that came with a salary of two thousand
five hundred francs a month – was for him a mixture of
boarding school and prison.

At the next desk, Moses was going over some figures,
reading them with eager eyes, the way a man in love might
read a letter from his mistress. He was the stereotype of a
rich young Jew, elegant, with a long nose set in a pale, delicate face. Whether he was tidying up the minutes of the
most recent AGM, keeping a record of the rise of the British
pound or the fall in the sugar cane market in Haiti, Moses
attacked his work with prodigious attention and enthusiastic
intensity. Yves envied him and he remembered what his boss
had told him once – he was also Jewish, but of old stock,
with a dark-grey beard and a nose that was almost unseemly:
'My dear Harteloup, what you're lacking is a drop, a very
tiny drop of our blood . . .'

Yves recalled the gesture of his soft, hairy hand, and his
Germanic accent: '. . . A trop, a ferry tiny trop . . .'

He smiled, but not happily.

Perhaps the old brute was right? It upset him that he
couldn't stop thinking about what had happened that day;
his weary mind was obsessed by them, like a silly tune that
you can't get out of your head, or fragments of a nightmare
that linger on when you're still half asleep.

Nervously he cracked his knuckles and muttered: '. . .
Bloody life . . .'

Then he called out, annoyed: 'Jeanne, come on now, is that bath ready?'

Jeanne padded into the room; she was slightly deaf so she came closer whenever anyone spoke to her. She had a face like a weasel and the tired, vacant, resigned expression of a working-class woman. 'Did you want me, Monsieur?'

'My bath.'

'But, Monsieur . . . Monsieur knows very well that the gas boiler broke down this morning . . .'

'You mean you didn't call the repair man?'

'But I did, Monsieur.'

'Well?'

'Well, he didn't come, Monsieur.'

Yves was about to start shouting abuse at her for being so stupid – he was hardly a patient man – but the sight of her calm, apathetic face made him feel ashamed. All he did was make a vague, weary gesture.

'All right then . . . fill up a tub for me . . . why did you let the fire go out?'

'I forgot,' she mumbled, kneeling down with difficulty to blow on the damp logs that were smoking but refused to burn.

'There's hardly any wood left,' she pointed out. 'Monsieur didn't leave me any money.'

'All right, all right,' he snapped.

He made do with two pails of water that Jeanne heated up in the kitchen; then he slipped on his pyjamas and sat down near the fireplace to have his lonely supper; Pierre lay at his feet, sleeping and panting quietly as he dreamed.

He ate his badly cooked soft-boiled eggs and a slice of galantine, then drank the glass of Montrachet that Jeanne brought him. She warned him that it was the last bottle and then he went up to bed. In the empty apartment, the clock sounded like a beating heart. Yves recalled how, when he was a very young man, he loved the peace and quiet of deserted rooms. That was a time when solitude intoxicated him like a powerful, bitter liqueur; but now, being alone aroused a vague feeling in him that resembled fear; in spite of himself, he sometimes imagined falling ill in the middle of the night, choking, gasping for breath, calling for help – in vain, since Jeanne would be fast asleep on the sixth floor. He was ashamed of his cowardice, yet he shivered involuntarily as he watched the darkness gathering in the corners of the room and the folds of the curtains. At such moments he truly understood why people got married . . . to have 'that something', a presence, the sound of skirts rustling, someone to whom you can tell insignificant things, someone you can scold for no apparent reason when you're in a bad mood, someone who is there when you are silent.

It was strange, though, that at such moments he never thought of Denise . . . To him, this affair was quite simply exhausting. He had to be tender, loving, passionate on cue; despite his worries over the thousand small everyday problems that plagued him like flies on a hot day, he had to whisper sweet nothings, smile, caress her. Even when he was suffering with a terrible migraine, he had to keep talking to avoid seeing Denise's anxious eyes, to block out her endless sad little questions: 'What's wrong? What are you thinking about? You love me, don't you?' She was a pretty young woman, kind and charming, made to laugh, to be happy, to love, not someone he would confide in about his endless sordid little problems. And besides, a mistress can always console a man in the throes of some lofty romantic anguish, he thought, but she wouldn't be able to stand it for long if she had to listen to her lover saying: 'Well, I need to find three hundred francs to pay my taxes. Jeanne forgot to get the boiler repaired again. The furniture is all dusty; the lace curtains are torn . . . I ought to replace the silk fabric on the armchair; it's starting to fray. But I don't have the time . . . I don't even have time to buy underwear, bedlinen, socks . . .' So he said nothing, or spoke of insignificant things, or even whispered those sweet nothings that weren't exactly lies, but which, because he felt obliged to say them, left him feeling dead with exhaustion . . .

'When I'm with her,' he thought with remarkable irritation, 'I always have to be mentally wearing a dinner jacket. That kind of thing is no longer part of my life, sadly . . .'

Then he remembered, with more resignation than eagerness, that she had promised to telephone him around ten o'clock. She would probably come to his place, pretending to be going to the theatre, or to a friend's house. He sighed. It was so strange . . . When he was sure he was going to see her he would put off their meeting until the very last moment: what he felt wasn't exactly boredom, rather the absence of desire. He wanted to delay the moment they were to meet; wandering the streets, he would invent a thousand excuses in order to be late; he was too confident that she would be waiting there, too sure of her tenderness, her love. Yet all it took was the slightest obstacle from Denise to make him feel he was in love again, anxious and full of pleasurable impatience; if Denise wasn't feeling very well he went mad, tormented himself, grew sweet and loving; he felt ill himself when she was ill; he couldn't leave her; she suddenly became more precious than anything else in the world. But when she felt better a few days later, he started dragging his love around with him again, as if it were a heavy burden.

That evening, as he waited for her to telephone, he sat down at the table, pushed Pierrot away – the dog kept nuzzling his dark, damp nose into Yves's hand – and with a resigned sigh began going through a pile of papers: bills, some paid, some due, tailors' reminders, Jeanne's accounts. Towards the end of the month he was always a few hundred francs short of what he really needed; and around the 20th of each month he forced himself to go through his accounts, which was complicated, took a long time and always left him in a bad mood because he realised he had once again broken the promise he'd made to himself to spend less money. With his two thousand five hundred francs monthly salary, some of his colleagues, married and with children, seemed to be able to get by easily. But from the 1st to the 30th of each month, Yves was regularly short of money. It is fair to say that he understood perfectly well why this happened and how expensive habits – taking taxis to work in the morning so he wouldn't be late, luxury cigarettes, clothes he could not really afford, leaving tips too often and too generously – seriously affected the balancing of his budget; he understood all this but didn't have the strength to stop; he preferred to deprive himself of necessities in order to have luxuries, yet he suffered because of it. He was not a bohemian at heart, he was no longer young enough to be carefree; only a twenty-year-old can get by on very little.

He sighed, pushed away the papers, put his head in his hands. It was past ten o'clock. Denise wouldn't be phoning. He felt more relieved than disappointed. At the back of the room the lamp lit up the turned-down bed with its white sheets; he imagined with delight the coolness of the linen, the soft pillow, how restful it would be to sleep alone, calmly, peacefully. Oh! To stretch out . . . to pull up the heavy green satin quilt, embroidered with golden bees, that had once belonged to his great-uncle, a Senator under the Second Empire . . . to light a cigarette, to reach over to the swivel table near his bed – inlaid with mother-of-pearl and tortoise-shell – and choose one of his favourite old books, one he had read and reread a thousand times, to leaf through it for a moment before switching off the light, turning towards the wall and . . . falling asleep . . . His eyes were heavy and painful . . . He opened them very wide, like a child who doesn't want to go to bed. The telephone rang. He picked up the receiver. It was Denise, of course.

'Yves, my darling, come and join us at the Perroquet in an hour, all right?'

'But don't you realise . . .' he started to say.

'Oh, do come along, Yves, please,' she begged. Her sad little voice sounded so disappointed, so humble that he felt sorry for her and rather ashamed.

'I must admit,' he thought, 'it's true; you'd think I was ninety-eight years old,' and, with a resigned sigh, he said: 'All right . . . See you soon, Denise . . .'

Pierrot wagged his tail and looked at him; then his bright

eyes turned longingly towards the bed as if to ask: 'Well? Why aren't you going to bed? It's late . . . you should put out the light and then I'll go and lie in my favourite spot, near the fire, on the animal skin that has such a wonderful smell of muskrat that you can't smell, no, because you're a man, an imperfect creature . . . the shimmering flames will dance up to the ceiling, then die out and I'll watch over you while you sleep . . . it will be just the two of us, all alone, peaceful . . .' But Yves was prowling around the cold apartment, his eyes burning with weariness, looking for various pieces of clothing in the wardrobes and in the dark recesses of the cupboards: his evening dress, silk socks, starched shirt front and long white crêpe de Chine scarf with his initials picked out in black, all of which Jeanne was determined to leave in a different place every week.

17

At the Perroquet, sitting on a red velvet divan, were the Jessaints, Yves, Madame Franchevielle and some English friends of the Jessaints, Mr and Mrs Clarke. The Englishman was a redhead, thin and lively; his wife was tall and slim with soft, light-blonde hair that was starting to grey; she had the strong, sunburned arms of a tennis player, sharp, brusque gestures and a shrill, birdlike voice.

They were passing through Paris and had arrived only the night before. They looked around the Perroquet with the naïve amazement of foreigners whose muddled admiration confuses the Louvre (museum and department stores), Notre Dame Cathedral and Pigall's in Montmartre.

The Perroquet was packed that night. What's more, it was an impressive sight: the room was larger than usual in such places, vast, airy, with high ceilings. And the women – it was still relatively early – could make their way comfortably around the room where multicoloured parrots displayed their bright feathers. All the women looked ravishing . . .

but only from a distance, from a very great distance; close up, on the other hand, it was astonishing to see how ugly they were, with a few rare exceptions: so withered beneath their painted faces, their feet tortured into shoes that were too narrow, plump backs, reddish arms impossible to hide despite the thick layer of powder. Yves watched them for a long time, feeling a kind of cruel delight as they danced, dresses halfway up their calves, their hair cut short like a young boy's, suddenly turning towards him, unsuspecting, the lying faces of old women. At the next table, one of those ageless Americans with sharp, skeletal shoulders, wearing a string of pearls that disappeared into the folds of her neck, was simpering as she rocked a doll dressed as Pierrot; beneath the powder and make-up, the pouches under her eyes were swollen and bulged hideously . . . Another woman, vaguely resembling a toad with her big head and a dwarfish body wrapped in the folds of a divine dress, was staring avidly and with the frightening tenderness of an ogress at a sad young boy; like two tentacles, her arms were wrapped round him, he looked stunned, terrified and resigned . . . Yves hated all these women, savagely, even though he didn't know them.

And besides, everything frustrated him, bored him, irritated him that evening – the shrill music of the jazz bands, the black musicians' frenzied fits of laughter, the little shrieks, the coy expression on the faces of these grandmothers in short dresses, all this stupid childishness, the forced cheerfulness, everything, even Denise, carefree, happy, expensive-looking in her silver shoes and white dress that shimmered softly under the lights; she was having fun, laughing, while he sat there furious, sad and tense, drinking without being thirsty, laughing without feeling like laughing, forced to smile and be polite, despite a secret, angry desire to see them all go to hell! Under the table he could feel Denise's slim leg reaching over to touch his; without thinking he returned the gentle pressure, while his eyes despairingly took in the collection of champagne bottles on the table, more numerous with each passing minute.

With a disagreeable little shudder he could already imagine the inevitable moment when, feigning indifference, he would reluctantly have to ask Jessaint or Mr Clarke: 'Tell me, my friend, how much do I owe you?' Then would come the polite refusal, his insistence, the offhand reply – a figure that represented a quarter of his monthly salary; he would smile, take out his wallet and throw down a few hundred-franc notes for the maître d' and casually light up a cigarette . . . In the past month there had been five of these little celebrations . . .

The woman selling dolls passed by, displaying her basket of cute little toy men and women dressed in various costumes: Pierrots, characters from the *commedia dell'arte*, Spanish dolls with enormous velvet frills and flounces. Mrs Clarke, Madame Franchevielle and Denise reached for them: these toys for adults were enormously popular. Jessaint bought three of them.

Denise turned towards Yves: 'Oh, do get one for Francette!' she cried out impulsively.

Without flinching, Yves took out his wallet. Then she changed her mind, blushed, tried to stop him from paying, stammered, grew flustered as he stretched out his hand, gave the woman two hundred-franc notes and told her to keep the change. Then he smiled and handed the doll to Denise; but she recognised only too well the cold, forced smile he put on when he was in a bad mood, the hard look in his eyes and the evil, stubborn, sad expression. She realised she had wounded his sensitive pride, clumsily reminding him that he was poor. (As if life didn't do that at every moment of the day!) It wasn't her fault, though: she'd acted impulsively; she couldn't get used to the idea that two miserable hundred-franc notes might possibly be a large sum to anyone . . . Nevertheless she felt like kicking herself . . . She grew all meek and withdrawn, but quickly saw that such modest behaviour annoyed him even more; she began to flirt, whispered softly to him, glanced up at him through her long eyelashes; he replied with stiff politeness.

Little by little, her cheerfulness, her liveliness, turned sour. It was always the same. At first she was happy to show him off . . . other women clearly admired his sophistication and attractive physique . . . she was happy to say quietly over and over again with secret, passionate pride: 'He's mine . . . mine . . .'; then, gradually, for one reason or another, her heart would grow heavy, weighed down by a vague feeling of anxiety, the noise bothered her, she was tired of dancing . . . she felt unhappy, sometimes so unhappy that she had to force back the absurd, bitter tears that rose up in her throat and choked her. She wanted to look into Yves's eyes and see concealed tenderness there, suppressed desire on his lips . . . Other couples felt close, together, even in a crowd . . . But they . . . they were far, so far from one another. Other people always destroyed their illusion of intimacy – so rare, so precious – that her patient, caring hands sometimes managed to create, but it was as fragile as antique lace . . .

Was it her fault or his? She didn't know: she lowered her head.

All around her the sad, wild music of the black jazz musicians rang out, resonant with both tears and laughter . . . 'the tears of a clown', Denise thought vaguely . . . At certain moments when she felt inconsolable, the low beating of the bass drum played by the black musician with shiny white teeth tore at her heart more keenly, more cruelly, than a bow in the hands of a virtuoso . . . A new set began; the dishevelled women forgot to powder their shiny noses and sweaty cheeks; a little flame gleamed in the half-closed eyes of the men; and the slightly tipsy couples stopped dancing, swaying on the spot as they pressed their twitching bodies together. A vague, stupefying feeling of boredom fell over everyone. Madame Franchevielle was smoking, leaning on the table, without taking any notice of the colourful streamers that men aimed at her as they passed. Mrs Clarke and Jessaint talked about golf, hockey and polo. Yves sat in silence, pensively stirring his champagne with a wooden swizzle stick. Only Mr Clarke, who was fairly drunk, was having a wonderful time; his face was flushed and he'd put a pink paper hat on his head; he began to flirt with Denise in his funny, incorrect French, using naïve words that barely concealed his eager, fierce desire. She let him talk, hardly listening; in a quiet, angry whisper, she wished he would die. The music kept playing, the dancers swayed on the spot, the women's jewellery sparkled under the bright lights.

'All this luxury is rather nice,' said Jessaint, who had rather questionable taste.

He turned towards Yves who replied with feeling: 'No, it's reprehensible and mad.'

Then he thought better of it and forced a slight smile. In the past he had found all this completely natural, enjoyable, but that was a time when he could join in the party. Now he played at being a moralist . . . Although it wasn't really a game, he thought . . . A kind of disgust, of bitter weariness, had settled in his heart for several years now, since the war . . . ? It had persisted . . . 'like the petty world-weariness of nineteenth-century authors', his thoughts ran on, 'their *mal du siècle*, but without the Romantic gloss'.

Everyone around him was talking now. The Clarkes wanted to round off the evening by going to Montmartre and then Les Halles. They decided to start with a Russian cabaret.

'Are you coming?' Denise whispered to Yves.

Yves bit his lip as he worked out with remarkable accuracy the money he had already spent.

His wallet was completely empty. He shook his head. 'Denise, I have a terrible migraine . . .'

She began begging him: to part on this note of silent sulkiness, to be forced to remember his cold expression, his sullen replies until the next day! She simply didn't have the strength . . . She went pale.

'Please, I'm begging you . . .'

'Oh!' he murmured quietly. He was tense, on edge. She thought that perhaps he was jealous of Clarke's attentions.

'You're not upset because of that fool, are you?' she asked.

He nearly started laughing. 'Of course not, really . . .'

Such disdain wounded her, as if he had slapped her in the face. She blushed.

'Don't come, then . . . In fact, I'd prefer if you didn't . . . You always spoil things for me whenever I'm happy . . .'

Her voice was husky, full of tears. He leaned in towards her with an icy gesture of apology. 'I know I do, believe me . . . I'm terribly sorry.'

They went outside; it was raining hard, the water pounding the pavement; a sharp wind whipped the flames of the gaslights in the street.

'Can we drop you off at your place?' asked Jessaint as the sleek, shiny black car approached; it glistened even more under the rain.

Yves, detecting a slight tone of pity in Jessaint's voice, was seriously tempted to refuse; but he glanced down at his patent-leather shoes and imagined himself chilled to the bone, soaked, ridiculous-looking in his Inverness cape and silk hat, running through the downpour trying in vain to find a taxi, and so, like a coward, he accepted.

After they had dropped him at his front door and the car headed off towards Pigalle, Clarke asked: 'Why didn't Harteloup come with us?'

Jessaint shrugged; *he* understood very well what his spoiled child of a wife found so hard to comprehend.

'He hasn't got a penny, the poor devil,' he said, laughing unconsciously, the way a rich man does, aware of who he is and satisfied with himself and his wealth. 'It's a shame; he's as proud as a peacock! And he's not really a bad sort. All the same, he should have understood that we wouldn't have let him pay . . .'

Suddenly Denise complained that she needed some air, rolled down the window and leaned out, in spite of the rain, her face very red. She hated her husband because he pitied her lover. Through the opening at the top of her coat, her hands nervously gripped the diamond necklace she was wearing; the light from an electric street lamp suddenly shone into the car, a flash of bright pink; the diamonds sparkled in the darkness. Denise clenched her teeth. She would have liked to pull off all her jewellery, throw it at Yves and say: 'Take them, only smile . . .' But can happiness be bought?

Yet at the same time she resented him for it; it made her feel ashamed, but she did resent him for it. Why wasn't he the most handsome, the most wonderful man in the world, the wealthiest? He was a man, he was the man she loved; she needed to admire him, respect him, and she wanted everyone else to admire and respect him as well . . . But they felt sorry for him. She angrily bit her lip.

'What's the matter, Denise?' Jessaint asked her with affectionate concern, taking her hand. 'You've gone completely white.'

'Oh, leave me alone,' she cried, sounding almost hateful.

He sat back, surprised and frightened. Then she raised the collar of her coat to hide her face, pretending she was cold; she could feel the anguished tears falling from her eyes, flowing slowly down towards the corners of her mouth, leaving a bitter taste. She shuddered at the thought that in a few minutes everyone would see her in the bright lights with her red eyes and the silvery trail of tears down her powdered cheeks. Yet she couldn't stop crying; the tears flowed and flowed, disappearing into the silk bodice of her dress and among the diamonds of her necklace.

18

Something was definitely wrong . . . Denise could sense it that morning.

She was still in bed: it was just before nine o'clock. She took the mirror from her bedside table and looked at herself for a long time with that anxious expression unique to women who are getting older or are unhappy. She was right: something was definitely wrong. Pensively she traced a barely perceptible line at the left side of her mouth with her finger, as if trying to wipe it away; it wasn't a wrinkle, but it wasn't a dimple either, unfortunately! It was just the hint of a line and it troubled her, like some secret warning . . .

Another bad night, with an almost physical sense of heaviness, there, on her chest, and those horrible, upsetting dreams in which her lover was taken far away from her, dreams that woke her in tears. She sighed. How long ago they seemed now, those glorious mornings in Hendaye, when their love was so new! She even thought affectionately back to the calm days of the past when simply the absence of pain could pass

for happiness, like a continuation of the peace you feel in childhood. But now she had distanced herself – willingly or not
– from her husband, her daughter, her friends . . . She realised in terror that, in fact, all she had in the world – in the
entire world! – was Yves. Perhaps that was the reason she
clutched on to him with a kind of frustrated frenzy. Love
born from fear of solitude is as sad and powerful as death.
Her desire for Yves, his physical presence, his words, was
becoming a kind of bleak madness. When they were apart,
she tortured herself wondering what he was doing, whom
he was with, where he was. When she leaned back in his
arms, the suffering she would feel the next day gradually ate
away at her happiness like a slow poison. In her heart, even
in the heat of his caresses, she thought always of how quickly
time was passing, how very quickly (could this be their last
time together?) . . . Sometimes, when the clock chimed
seven, she would cling to him so tightly, pale and trembling,
as if she were drowning, that it would frighten him. And
when she tried to explain what she was feeling, he would
sigh and say 'my poor darling . . .' and stroke her face, as
if she were a sick child. But he didn't understand a woman's
need for security, that frantic desire for his presence and the
terror of losing him, as if nothing else in the world could
possibly exist without him.

Yet even those moments of sharp, intense pain were rare.
Most of the time their affair – like the affairs of three-quarters
of the illicit couples in Paris – was limited to brief encounters
between six and seven o'clock in the evening, when Yves
got off work, filled with meaningless conversation, a few
frustrated embraces . . . Saturdays: afternoons of loving

moments, of silences, the introspective, disagreeable mask of the man removed as he takes his mistress, the way you drink wine, selfishly . . . So little, so little . . . monotony, boredom, anxiety, sadness, interspersed with sharp, intense pain, and then, boredom, anxiety once more . . . so little, so very little joy . . . She lowered her head, defeated . . . Last summer, at the beach, Francette sometimes amused herself by plunging both hands in the sea to try to catch a bit of foam; she would press her hands tightly together and squeal with delight; then she would run over to Denise as fast as her little legs would carry her; but when she opened her hands there was nothing left but a bit of water . . . So she would cry, poor thing . . . Then she would start all over again . . . And that was exactly what love was like.

It was a sun-drenched June morning. To avoid seeing the blue sky, the young trees, the light of this beautiful day that was like an insult to her misery, Denise buried her head in the warm darkness of the pillow. But a gentle tapping at the door made her start.

'Who is it?' she called out.

The calm voice of her mother replied: 'It's me, my darling.'

Denise quickly composed herself, got out of bed and rushed to open the door. Madame Franchevielle was standing in the doorway, looking bright, young, exquisitely made-up and wearing perfume.

'Still in bed, you lazy girl! I've come to take you to lunch . . .' she said with a smile.

Denise, who was not terribly eager to face her mother's knowing looks, mumbled: 'I'd love to . . . but . . . I was just about to go out . . . and . . . I'm sorry, Mama . . .'

She was standing in front of her mother in her pyjamas, barefoot, absent-mindedly pushing the dark strands of hair off her forehead. She was very pale and shivered slightly.

Madame Franchevielle looked at her more closely. 'Are you ill, Denise?' she asked anxiously.

'No, I'm not . . . not at all . . .'

Her faint voice sounded utterly exhausted.

Madame Franchevielle took Denise's face in her hands. 'Denise, what's wrong?'

Denise shook her head, pressing her lips together so as not to cry.

Madame Franchevielle gently stroked her hair. 'My dear child, are you in pain?'

No reply. Then, with deliberate harshness, she looked deep into her daughter's eyes and asked: 'Is Yves cheating on you?'

Denise didn't even protest. A sad little smile appeared on her trembling mouth. 'You think you're shocking me, Mama? I know that you're very intelligent – even too intelligent! . . . And besides, I can't hide much, if anything, I'm afraid . . .'

'He's not cheating on you?' her mother repeated stubbornly.

'No.'

'Does he love you?'

'Ah! Now there's the question . . .'

Her voice was hoarse. She made a pleading gesture.

'Mama, leave me be, just leave me be, you can't help me . . .'

She had gone over to the window, turning her back on her mother, and pressed her warm mouth against the glass.

Then two arms lovingly embraced her. 'Denise, don't you trust your mama any more?'

In the past, just saying those few words and softly stroking her forehead, the way you would calm a young headstrong animal, Madame Franchevielle had always managed to soothe Denise's childhood tantrums, just as she did later with all her adult problems. Defeated once more, Denise told her everything . . . Her anxieties, her inexplicable suffering and, especially, how depressed she felt for no real reason, the mysterious shadows that hovered over their love, like the wispy clouds of summer, when you're by the sea, clouds that spread from one end of the sky to the other, as far as you can see, and that finally block out the sun . . .

'You think he doesn't love you?' asked Madame Franchevielle tentatively, making sure to soften the cutting tone of her voice.

'I don't know . . . I'm afraid . . .'

'But are you sure that you love him the way you should?'

'What are you saying, Mama?' Denise exclaimed forcefully, indignantly. 'I give him everything . . . my whole life . . . all my thoughts . . . even more . . . Look, when I wake up, even before I'm completely conscious, I feel something like a shock, deep inside me . . . the way I felt Francette, you know, when I was pregnant with her . . . and it's so painful, yet so sweet, just as it was then . . . It's almost as if I'm carrying my love inside me, like a child . . . You can't know what it's like, Mama . . .'

'I do know, my little one, I do know . . .'

'When I'm not with him I feel dead . . . it can't be called living . . . time drags by so slowly, pointlessly . . . You can't know what it's like . . .'

'But I do, I know only too well . . .'

'You do?' Denise asked, lowering her voice, just as her mother had when she asked the question. 'Have you . . . been in love, Mama? Well, then, explain it to me . . . why am I so unhappy? I have a handsome lover who is young and faithful, any woman's dream really . . . And yet I'm suffering . . . Look at me. I'm uglier, I know it. Why? Is love really a sickness, or am I "inventing bogeymen" as Francette would say when she tells herself fairy tales about wicked witches, "to scare myself"?'

Madame Franchevielle shook her head thoughtfully. 'It seems to me that your sickness has a name: egotism . . .'

'You mean his?'

'Yours as well . . .'

Denise gave a start.

'Now, if you listen to me without getting annoyed, you'll see that I'm right. Try to imagine, for example, how different your states of minds are when you meet? There's you, who have had nothing to worry about since morning apart from choosing which dress might please him the most, and him, preoccupied, tired, bored, tense, having worked hard all day long just to make ends meet . . . You're a spoiled child; do you have any idea what that must be like? And you're surprised there are problems! Egotist . . . Ah! Being in love is a luxury, my darling . . .'

Denise thought about this, nervously wringing her hands.

'But, Mama,' she finally said, 'what you're telling me I've often thought myself . . . Listen, though . . . My chamber-maid has a lover, a mechanic. He works all day long and harder than Yves; but in the evening he goes to her room on the sixth floor and they're happy together . . . And what about all the others, so many of them, all the other men! My husband, our friends, all of them! The time for the kind of heroes you find in Bourget's novels is gone, men who collected women and ties and had nothing better to do. Nothing better to do! Bourget's heroes would starve to death now . . .'

'No, they would work and some of them would be very unhappy. Harteloup will never get used to getting up every day at seven-thirty, waiting for a bus at the corner, in the rain, doing calculation, economising, being told what to do . . . It's not his fault. You talk about the others, your husband? Yet you're cheating on him . . . Yves seems cowardly to you . . . Perhaps he is. But you love him.'

Denise had stopped listening. She slowly shook her head and murmured: 'My love should feel like a kind of luxury he's rediscovered . . .'

'Who knows? Perhaps that is exactly the reason why it causes him such embarrassment? Like a visitor who is over-dressed in a shabby room? And you ask such different things of love. Good Lord! *Your* life has always been so peaceful, so pleasant, so secure . . . Of course you need the excitement of love, extraordinary pleasures, new kinds of pain, and words, words, words . . .'

'And what about him? What does he need?'

'Quite simply, peace.'

'Mama, what should I do?'

'Ah, what should you do? Love him less, perhaps? An excess of love is a great mistake, sometimes brings great suffering . . . My poor child . . . How difficult this all seems, doesn't it? But that's life . . . You will learn from life, just the way I did . . . Men don't want to be loved too much, you know . . . Listen, I'll tell you what made me understand that for the first time . . . Your poor little brother died . . . Do you still remember him, Denise?'

'I was so young . . . You loved him so much.'

'I adored him, Denise, as you can only adore a son . . . There's a kind of wonder at this little man you've made . . . You can't understand. He was my firstborn, my son . . . he was so beautiful . . . I was mad about him . . . I spent all my time stroking him, cuddling him, smothering him with kisses . . . One day, he was two and a half, the poor angel – he died three months later – I was hugging him frantically, and he pushed my arms away with both tiny hands and said: "Mama, you're loving me too much, you're suffocating me . . ." He was already a man, Denise.'

Denise said nothing. Then she gave a hard, humourless little laugh and spoke with difficulty.

'Everything you're telling me . . . do you know what it makes me think, Mama? The wisest thing to do would be to cheat on Yves, since I haven't the strength to give him up, or to love him less . . . This love that's suffocating him, as you put it, if I shared that love between two men, it would be just right . . . It's funny, it's monstrous, but that's the way it is . . .'

Madame Franchevielle shook her head. 'I once knew a woman,' she whispered, staring off into the distance, 'a woman who loved her lover just the way you love yours: madly, like the most wretched woman imaginable . . . She tormented him with her embraces, her anxieties, her jealous tenderness . . . And since she truly gave him everything – her whole heart, her whole life – she always felt as if she got nothing in return. You know very well that when it comes to love, both people feel as if they've made a fool's bargain, where the other always wins. They both forget the third player, that scoundrel: love . . . And so, both of them suffered . . . Then one day . . .'

'One day?'

'Well, one day the woman took a friend, toyed with him, to pass the time. He wasn't her lover. The idea of being physically unfaithful was unbearable to her. He was a friend. And she played at making him fall in love with her. She'd started out half-heartedly, doing just enough to take out her anxiety on some innocent man; then, little by little, she began to enjoy it . . . She became beautiful again. When a woman is happily in love she looks wonderful. Her lover noticed. He let her know it. Feeling guilty, she was more indulgent towards him, then, gradually, more indifferent, while he was happier . . . There you have it . . . That's all.'

Denise looked up. 'Where is this woman now, Mama?'

'Oh, she's gone, my darling, long gone . . .'

'Is she . . . is she still happy?'

'As much as anyone can be, at least . . . She had learned one of life's lessons: give very little and expect even less in return . . .'

'And she never misses the time when she was just an awkward young woman in love? She never regrets having suffered?'

Madame Franchevielle looked blankly away and said nothing. Then she let out a brief sigh and hesitated for a moment. But at last she replied.

'No,' she said firmly, 'never.'

19

Towards the end of June, Yves had serious problems: he got into debt and, in order to catch up a bit, he played the Stock Market, following the advice of Moses, his colleague at work. He never understood how, in the space of two weeks, the same transactions earned the young Jew several thousands of francs while he *lost* at least the same amount. He was forced to go to moneylenders, got into more trouble and finally ended up doing what he should have done in the beginning: he wrote to Vendômois, told him everything and begged for his help.

These were dark days for him. Worried and harassed, he found himself in exactly the same state of mind as a sick dog who lies down in a dark corner to suffer. Sometimes he even hated being with Denise, hated her physical presence; his poor, distraught soul wanted only peace. Too proud to share his problems with her, he remained stubbornly silent. And she didn't dare question him, for she had already learned, to her cost, that nothing in the world could force him to admit anything once he'd made up his mind not to.

Once he even fell asleep in her arms.

All night long he had paced back and forth in his room, trying to work out how long it would take until he finally got a reply from Finland. Moreover, the idea that Vendômois might be put in an awkward financial position because of him – might possibly go into debt himself – that idea haunted him, filled him with remorse. But what wounded his own masculine pride most deeply was to find that he was so helpless in the battle he faced every day; no matter how cowardly he thought himself, he couldn't help turning pale or stop his teeth from chattering at the idea of what would happen if Vendômois didn't come to his aid. Towards morning he was less agitated. Then, as the dawn light flickered outside his windows, he felt horribly depressed, as if his soul had left his body. It was a hideous sensation, similar to that flash of dizziness just before you faint . . . He pressed both hands against his chest; the wild beating of his heart was painful. Then he walked over to the window and opened it; the cool morning air felt good; he leaned on the sill and stayed there for a long moment without moving, without thinking. Little by little, day broke; the sky was all pink; the birds sang at the tops of their voices in the trees of a neighbouring garden. A car drove past on the deserted road and the sound of its horn echoed for a long time through the empty streets as all of Paris slept. The city was slowly coming to life.

Yves leaned out of the window and stared blankly at the pavement below. His entire body was trembling. Just a small effort . . . fall . . . end it all . . . it was very simple. His thoughts were painful and hazy, as in a dream. Fragments of memories floated through his mind, old, very old memories, the kind of memories that make you wonder if you aren't actually dreaming . . . The beautiful mornings of his childhood, cool mornings in unexplored towns he'd travelled through, and then the wartime mornings. It was only there that he stopped himself, stood up straight, wiped his forehead with a trembling hand. He had been a soldier. A soldier doesn't die that way. He forced his eyes closed so he wouldn't see the street or its pink paving stones in the early morning light and, keeping his eyes tight shut, he quickly closed the window. The horrible moment of weakness had passed; he started to feel alive again, or rather, the habit of living took hold of him once more. He mechanically followed his normal routine: he washed, shaved, got dressed, then went out.

It was already very hot; it was the beginning of a beautiful summer's day; women's faces peered over the balconies; street sellers passed by with their little carts full of flowers, shouting: 'Roses! Who wants some beautiful roses!'; tiny fountains of water from hosepipes sprayed from one side of the pavement to the other, glistening like liquid rainbows; young children went past on their bicycles, chasing each other and singing loudly; they had wicker baskets on their backs and their smocks fluttered in the wind. Yves tried hard to notice every last detail in the street, just as a sick man desperately tries to concentrate on the countless little things in his bedroom. Gradually he felt comforted, Lord knows why! The more he breathed in the cool air of that Paris morning, still relatively clean and fresh, the more a semblance of peace returned to his heart. The horrible despair of the night before seemed out of proportion to his problems; he felt ashamed. He walked past a public garden, a patch of green with an ugly statue in the middle; it was almost empty; they had just opened the gates; he went in and sat down for a moment. A young man and woman, employees in a shop, no doubt, walked slowly down the path. The man was intently telling her something. His girlfriend listened; she had a plain face but it was lit from within by a sort of warm emotional glow. Yves thought the man must be complaining about something unfair that had happened to him, or explaining his problems; she said nothing, she couldn't help him, but she suffered with him and, because of that, the man's burden was lightened. 'He's a happy man,' thought Yves. 'He can put the weight of his troubles on his companion's shoulders.' He recalled Denise's anxious face; he imagined confiding in her. But no. What was the point? The humble working-class man was fortunate: he simply shared both his sadness and his joy with his woman . . . He stood up, his face darker once more. The garden was starting to fill up with nannies and children. He realised he'd be late for work. Almost running, he headed for the nearest metro.

That evening, around seven o'clock, Denise came to see Yves. He opened the door for her, as usual; she was shocked by the way he looked: he seemed thinner, gaunt, with ashen cheeks; his eyes were red and swollen from not sleeping and looked as if they were burning. She quickly took his hand: 'What's wrong . . . my darling?'

'Nothing, nothing at all,' he said, shaking his head and forcing a smile.

She made an impatient gesture, then composed herself. How resolutely he kept her out of his life . . . Perhaps he was cheating on her after all? Did he really have so many problems? Was he simply in a bad mood, as he so often was? How could she tell? Did she really know him? 'Can anyone really know anyone else?' she thought despondently.

They had gone into Yves's bedroom. She automatically walked over to the round mirror hanging on the wall in its antique wood gilt frame, where she had taken off her hat and later put it back on again so many times since last autumn. She looked at her serious face, then started to smooth down her boyish hair with the gentle movement of a cat washing itself, as Yves had once described it. Meanwhile Yves had sat down in a large armchair that faced the window. When Denise turned round she saw him sitting there, motionless, eyes closed. She quietly took a cushion and sat down at her lover's feet. Yves's hand was resting on his knee. Denise pressed her cheek against it, then her lips. But Yves didn't say a word, didn't move: he was asleep.

Denise looked at him, dumbstruck, vaguely wondering if it was some game; then she rested her head against the arm of the chair and stared out of the window, patiently waiting for Yves to open his eyes. Outside, night was falling, a wonderfully sweet June evening. Denise looked up, trying to see the watery green crescent moon that was beginning to take shape, like a silvery sign against the pale sky. A delicate pink haze blurred the clear night air; it grew imperceptibly darker; night fell, transparent as dusk.

'Yves,' Denise whispered.

The room grew dark; Yves's face, tilted backwards in the

shadows, took on the peaceful seriousness of the dead. Without knowing why, Denise was afraid. She pulled herself up on to her knees to see him better. He was fast asleep. She straightened up so she was at the same level as he was, then studied him closely once more. There was something tense, mistrustful about the way he slept. So many times, after they'd made love, she had watched him sleep, and always she had the same painful, maddening impression that he was a mystery to her. And never as much as today. She leaned forward so she was nearly touching him; she had to resist the cruel, childish desire to force open his sleepy eyelids so she might catch hold of the end of his dream; but his eyes remained stubbornly closed, the lids dark from lack of sleep; and then he began to breathe heavily, the way you do in the middle of a nightmare.

She gently shook him. He shuddered violently and looked at her with an anguished, lost expression; the window cast a wide, milky patch through the dark room.

'Is it very late?' he asked in a muffled tone of voice.

He saw Denise frowning as she stared at him. He tried to smile and made an effort to stroke her hair. As often happens if you fall asleep during the day, he felt worn out, crushingly tired. He couldn't think straight: it was as if part of him were still asleep . . .

Then Denise lowered her eyes and spoke very quickly: 'Listen, listen to me, Yves . . . I can't do this any more . . . I don't want to do this any more . . . Why did you fall asleep? You didn't sleep last night, did you? Where were you? Tell me . . . I'd rather know . . . Is there someone else? No, don't laugh. How am I supposed to know? Maybe you're in love with a woman who wants nothing to do with you? Perhaps you're suffering because of another woman? Yves, take pity on me . . . I'm begging you, begging you . . . take pity on me . . .'

Yves shrugged his shoulders. This really was too much.

'I swear that it's not what you think, my poor darling,' he said softly, in the measured, overly calm tone of voice you use when talking to sick children.

'Well, then, are you worried about money?' she asked brusquely.

He was about to say 'yes' but then . . . he noticed the string of pearls she was wearing. He knew her very well; she would hand him the pearls and say 'Take them', or some other sweet, mad thing like that. And, to tell the truth, it was really quite simple. She had ten times the money to save him, ten times . . . He bit his lip so hard that it bled; he knew why he said nothing; he knew very well why. Oh! If only she were as poor as he was! But deep inside lurked the vague fear that he wouldn't have the strength to push away her outstretched hand, her necklace, her money, her charity . . .

He shook his head again. 'No.'

'So I can't help you?' asked Denise with a kind of despair.

'No,' he said again, quietly, showing no emotion in his voice.

Then, suddenly, he placed a tentative hand on Denise's hair and stroked it gently, for a long time.

'Denise, do you really want to help me? Then listen. I need to be alone. What can I say? It's not my fault . . . When I'm in pain I need to suffer alone, absolutely alone, like a dog. It helps me . . . I don't want to see you suffering because of me, because of my problems that are neither as serious nor as terrible as you may think. No, really! They'll get resolved and very soon. All I'm asking you for is a few days, just a few days . . . But I must be alone, Denise, completely alone . . . Take pity on me . . . Otherwise I'll go mad! Your reproaches, your suffering . . . I can't do this any more either, Denise, I can't . . . Give me some time to work out my problems, to mull them over and then sleep them off, like wine . . . Then things will be better . . . I'll be well again. Think of me as ill or mad, but just let me be alone!'

As he talked, he had begun to sound more and more agitated, and at that very moment he truly desired solitude, the way a sick man longs for cool water or a piece of fruit. His hands and mouth were trembling.

Denise turned pale and stood up. She powdered her face and put on her hat. She said nothing; she didn't even look at him. He felt a vague sense of remorse, tinged with fear.

'Denise,' he murmured more gently, 'I'll call you, all right?'

'As you please,' she replied.

She didn't dare look at him: she was afraid she might burst into tears. He had hurt her more than if he had actually hit her. But did he even understand? He had rejected her, sent her away . . . a savage undercurrent of resentment ran through her wounded, loving heart. Seeing how calm she was, however, he simply thought: 'She understands.' She stretched her hand out to him in silence.

He kissed it, then pulled her close, held her tightly and kissed her cheek; she just stood there, motionless. He wanted to kiss her on the lips. She gently pushed him away and walked towards the door.

'Is it all right, then? I'll call you . . . in a few days?'

'Fine,' she murmured, 'fine . . . don't worry.'

She left.

Once alone, he felt a moment of enormous distress. He even made a move towards the door. Then he changed his mind. 'What's the point?' He sighed and went back over to the window. He saw her walking away, very quickly. Men watched her go by. She turned the corner and disappeared.

Then he called Pierrot and sat down with him in a big armchair. It was dark, silent . . . a kind of bitter peace flowed through him . . .

20

Two days passed without Denise seeing Yves or having any word from him.

On Saturday morning Jessaint suggested that he and his wife take the car and spend a few days in the countryside, as they often did, in a house they owned near Étampes; a hundred and fifty years ago it had been a wealthy tax collector's hideaway. Denise, who loved the countryside, was always happy to go there with her husband. This time, however, she refused, without even bothering to make up an excuse: she was sure that Yves would phone her some time during the day.

Jessaint did not insist. For a while now he seemed embarrassed and unhappy whenever he spoke to his wife; he guessed she was hiding some secret from him, thought Denise. But he undoubtedly preferred not to delve too deeply into that secret, whatever it might be. He felt the kind of shame and nervousness that people who are fundamentally honest feel when faced with others who lie and cheat. So he kissed Denise on the forehead, sighed a little and left on his own. And that resigned sigh coming from such a good, solid man, who could nevertheless be passionate at times, made an insidious little wound in Denise's heart, one of those wounds that barely hurts at first, but which slowly and surely grows more painful with time.

She had done absolutely nothing to prevent him from going. Their marriage was imperceptibly coming apart, like a knot made of two different bits of string that gradually grow thin and come apart. She was perfectly aware of this. The feeling of despondency that gripped her was rather similar to the helplessness you feel in a dream, when you stand by and do nothing as your house burns down, for example, as if it belonged to someone else.

After Jessaint had gone, she went to see Francette. She hugged her tight and asked how she was feeling: she thought she looked pale and thin, even though the little girl was as plump as a peach. She showered kisses on her baby arms and bare legs under the short white dress; she wanted to know how she had got every bruise and scratch on her knees and rosy elbows. For a moment she was tempted to send the nanny away and take care of France herself all day. Everyone says that small children can heal many wounds . . . And the room was so bright, so cheerful. On the table, Francette's fat black cat was sleeping in the sunlight; when he saw Denise, he deigned to stand up, arched his back, then stretched each long, velvety paw in front of him, one after the other, spreading his claws . . .

But Francette had been given a new scooter the day before; she quickly broke free from her mother's arms and ran to get her toy. Denise realised she would probably be preoccupied with it for the rest of the day: Francette devoted herself to all her games with a kind of passion. Denise wanted to sit her on her lap and tell her a story, keep her close for a while longer, to feel the sweet warmth of her little body. But all she managed to do was make her burst into tears of rage: little Mademoiselle France was very strong-willed. Denise had to leave.

All day long she waited; but Yves did not come to see her, nor did he give any sign of life. Late that evening Denise was still waiting by the phone, her head in her hands. Around midnight she threw herself down on the bed and fell into a fitful sleep. The next day was very beautiful, so she sent Francette and her nanny to have lunch at the Pré-Catelan in the Bois de Boulogne, then began desperately trying to think of what she could do all day to keep herself busy. All her friends had gone away: it was the time of year when Parisians pour out of the city en masse from Saturday until Monday; Madame Franchevielle was already in Vittel, as she was every year. When she thought about spending the afternoon all alone, Denise felt something akin to terror. As often happened, her determined feeling of hope had suddenly given way to despair; she no longer expected the promised phone call; or, at least, she wanted to try not to wait for it any longer. A thousand times she was tempted to write to Yves, or go to see him, to talk to him. But an irrational fear took hold of her at the idea of disobeying him. She knew him so well. If he felt she was badgering him when he had begged her to leave him alone, he was capable, she thought, of abruptly ending their affair. He had such a strange, oversensitive nature, how could anyone know what he might do? She knew only too well that there was only one thing she could do: wait patiently, as he had asked, until he had slept off his worries, whatever they might be, the way you sleep off too much wine.

There was so much difference between a man's pain, which could be appeased by solitude, and her own loving heart! My God, if anything terrible happened to her, Yves's presence, a simple word or gesture from him would be enough to console her, to make her happy . . . But, what could she do? This was what he was like . . . The resentment she had first felt towards him when he sent her away had dissolved into vague, bitter resignation. This was how it was. She had all the willing blindness that comes with love. In a kind of frenzy, she started thinking about what she could do that day. For she simply couldn't face being alone, all alone, in the empty apartment. She telephoned several friends, but no one was in Paris. Then, suddenly, she remembered the conversation she'd had with her mother a little while ago. She could hear herself saying: 'The wisest thing to do would be to cheat on Yves . . . This love that's suffocating him, as you put it, if I shared that love between two men, it would be just right.'

She was standing in the middle of the sitting room; the sun, like a golden mist, filtered through the slats in the shutters, closed to keep out the dust and heat. Denise shook her head in anger: 'This can't go on, no, it just can't go on', she said over and over again. She caught sight of her pale face in the mirror and was almost afraid of the look in her eyes. 'I'm unhappy,' she said out loud and a swift, harsh sob shook her; but she didn't cry. She walked over to the window in a daze and pushed open the shutters, then stood there, overwhelmed with emotion, staring gloomily at the cobblestones that glistened in the bright sunlight. A small car had just stopped opposite her house. Leaning out a bit, she realised it was her cousin Jean-Paul. She started to ring for the servant to tell him she didn't want any visitors. But it was too late; the doorbell rang at almost exactly the same moment. She could hear Jaja's voice in the hall, then he appeared at the entrance to the sitting room.

'Are you alone, Denise?'

'As you can see.'

She looked disapprovingly at his delicate, boyish, slightly pointed face. He always teased her.

But this time he refrained from remarking on the dark circles under her eyes and how terrible she looked. All he said was: 'I ran into your husband yesterday morning as he was leaving Paris. He told me he was going to Étampes without you.'

'That's right. And what about you? What are you doing in Paris when it's so hot?'

Jaja hesitated; then he replied with the slight smile at the corner of his mouth that made irritable people want to slap him across the face. 'If I told you it was to see you, you probably wouldn't believe me, would you?'

'*Probably.*'

In spite of herself, when she was with Jaja, Denise found herself using the words and intonations she had used when she was fifteen, when she had amused herself by imitating the tone of voice and mannerisms of her young cousin, who was a schoolboy in Janson-de-Sailly back then.

Jaja forced a little laugh. 'You see.'

Denise walked over to the sofa and sat down.

'Would you like something to drink?'

'Definitely. Have them bring up some liqueurs, brandy and lots of ice.'

He sat down in his favourite spot, on some cushions on the floor.

'Do you remember how we used to make cocktails in the schoolroom, Denise, and then hide them in our desks?' he asked.

'I remember . . . It was our schoolroom in the house in the country . . .'

'We used to jump out of the window and run away in the grounds . . .'

'Do you remember that hollow old willow tree where we used to hide?'

'And the swing that creaked so loudly?'

'And the stream we went through twenty times a day because we loved getting our feet wet?'

'And the mill? Do you remember how we climbed the ladder straight up to the loft and hid behind the sacks of flour?'

'I was a tomboy. Francette is going to be like me . . .'

'Where is she?'

'At the Pré-Catelan.'

Jaja knew exactly what he was doing by calling up their childhood memories. Denise looked back on the most insignificant moments from the past with great affection. She had softened at once and Jean-Paul could see the amused, tender smile he knew so well spread across her face.

'Are you waiting for someone?' he asked softly.

She hesitated a moment, then said no.

'Would you like me to take you for a spin in the car?' he asked.

'Has your girlfriend dropped you, Jaja?'

'Mind your own business. Are you coming or not?'

'Where?'

'Wherever you like. We could get out of Paris.'

'No. What if we ran into someone we knew?'

'So what?'

'Jacques wouldn't be very happy. I refused to go with him yesterday, you see?'

'All right. Then somewhere in Paris? I know, we could go to the Bois and give your daughter a kiss.'

'I'd like that,' Denise agreed.

'Go and put on your hat and coat.'

Denise rang for her maid. While she was helping her on with her coat, Denise whispered: 'If anyone rings, say that I'll be home by dinner time and ask them to call back.'

'Don't worry Madame.'

Jean-Paul pretended to be avidly breathing in the scent from the bouquet of flowers on the table.

He turned round. 'Let's go; hurry up, out . . .'

They got into the car. Jean-Paul, who dearly loved his car, was proudly pointing out its merits.

'You'll see how she races up hills if we go as far as Saint-Cloud. And the ride is as smooth as can be . . . she's a real gem, Denise, honestly.'

Denise let the warm breeze whip across her face and said nothing. It was one of those marvellous Sundays in Paris when the blue sky stretches above the rooftops like a layer of brand-new silk, without even a hint of shade; the pavements were crowded with ordinary people who walked slowly by with peaceful expressions and delighted satisfaction written on their faces. Just from the way they strolled past without hurrying, you could tell it was their day off; they all felt that they deserved this beautiful day with its sunshine and the scent of roses because they had worked so hard all week long; they weren't very attractive, these good people, nor were they well dressed, but as they went by, their simple happiness and tranquillity seemed contagious. Denise began to smile as she watched them, and a very sweet, inexplicable sense of contentment ran through her.

Jean-Paul noticed her expression. 'You enjoy looking at all these faces, do you?' he said.

'Yes, I do . . . Jean-Paul, don't go so fast . . . I like looking at them, I don't know why . . .'

Jean-Paul slowed down. They were getting closer to the Bois de Boulogne; there were more and more people: stout women with jet-black hats, elderly women in silk dresses, men with gaunt faces worn out from thankless jobs, pale children, small girls in white smocks, young boys in sailor outfits . . . 'Blessed are the poor in spirit!' Denise thought; and that saying she had always known suddenly took on a subtle, deeper meaning when applied to these humble people who bravely accomplished their daily tasks.

'Since they amuse you, shall I take you to the Butte de Montmartre? I bet you've never been there. Only tourists know about those kinds of places these days . . .'

'I went to the Lapin Agile one night, with the Clarkes.'

'But you must see it in the daytime.'

'Really?'

'Definitely. Do you want to go? If we go to the Pré-Catelan, all you'll see are masses of lovely ladies in their expensive Hispano-Suizas, and Francette doesn't need you . . . she already has a suitor . . . she told me so. She has a boyfriend who gave her a lollipop. She took it and then went and gave it to another little boy. She's already a woman. We'd cramp her style . . .'

'I'm beginning to think you're right,' said Denise with a sigh. 'What can you do? That's life . . . She loves her scooter more than me now . . . Later on – and soon – it will be a man . . .'

'Anyone would think you're feeling blue, Denise.'

'No, not at all.'

Jean-Paul had already turned the car round. They were speeding towards Montmartre; for several minutes Jaja allowed himself the pleasure of racing madly through the city; they were soon within sight of the Lamarck metro station.

Jean-Paul stopped in front of a small café. He honked the horn repeatedly until the owner came out in his shirtsleeves.

'Well, hello there, Monsieur. Do you want to leave the car with me?'

'As usual.'

'Would Madame like a glass of wine?' the owner asked with a smile.

Denise, amused, agreed. The owner winked at Jean-Paul and whispered: 'Pretty little thing.'

'Aren't you worried about all these steps?'

'No, of course not.'

She climbed easily up the stairs; her light, full coat floated behind her, its graceful folds like antique drapery.

She stopped at the top of the steps to catch her breath. 'It's chilly, Jean-Paul . . .'

It was true. The breeze blowing at the top of Montmartre was virtually pure. Denise walked over to a railing that enclosed the small raised area where they were standing; she leaned over; a foggy mist hid the city stretched out beneath her feet, but the dome of Les Invalides shone through the golden haze, along with the delicate outline of the Eiffel Tower; Denise could hear a faint bustle and murmur from below.

Jaja walked over to her and they continued climbing the hill. Dark old houses and narrow alleyways basked in the sun; on each side of the steep pavement, spiked with pebble-stones, they could hear the crisp sound of little streams of cool water flowing past. Dogs with yellowish fur encrusted with mud slept in the middle of the road, without a care in the world.

'Have you ever seen dogs like that?' asked Jean-Paul, pointing to one of them; it looked like a cross between a basset hound, a spaniel and a mastiff.

'Only in drawings by that artist, Poulbot.'

'You're right . . . and the young girls over there, too,' said Jean-Paul, nodding towards a group of children running past, smocks billowing in the wind and hats fixed tightly on their pointy little heads.

In the Place du Tertre several families sat round wooden tables drinking grenadine. Jean-Paul and Denise sat down among them. The sky gradually grew paler; the faint scent of lilacs hovered in the air, as if they were in the countryside. A little girl in her communion dress walked by; in the fading sunlight, her white veil shimmered pink and gold. Two more, very serious-looking little girls followed behind in sky-blue dresses, paper flowers in their hair, each holding a single bright pink rose in full bloom. As soon as they had passed, the bells of Sacré Coeur began to ring out.

Jean-Paul ordered some sparkling wine; he said nothing now, just drank it slowly, raising his glass and watching the golden bubbles lit by the sun for a long time before bringing the glass to his lips.

'Do you come here often? You seem to know the place.'

'Every now and again . . .'

She was smiling, so he added, in a serious tone of voice: 'But I come alone . . .'

'Really.'

'It's true; it's a chance to have some peace . . . I get in my car, climb the hill, sit down here . . . and don't think about anything; I'm just happy . . .'

Denise looked at him, somewhat taken aback.

'What's so surprising?' he asked.

'You are. I thought you were always flying about, never staying put . . .'

'You shouldn't judge a book by its cover, my dear.'

He slowly emptied his glass, lit a cigarette and leaned back in his chair without saying a word. Denise was almost disappointed by his silence: she vaguely expected him to behave differently; but Jaja just sat there smoking, looking detached and slightly mocking. She poured herself some wine and quickly emptied her glass; it was light and refreshing. All around them the square was emptying out. The wonderful calm of the evening embraced them.

'It's so nice here,' Denise said out loud, half closing her eyes. The gentle breeze caressed her cheeks; the wine she had drunk made her feel rather dizzy and her arms and legs slightly heavy.

'So nice . . .' she said once more with a smile.

Then, suddenly, she thought: 'It's almost as if I'm not in so much pain . . .' Her surprise was accompanied by the instinctive anxiety you can't help but feel when you've been injured, for example, and then suddenly realise that it doesn't hurt any more.

'It's really strange, but I'm not in so much pain . . .'

She breathed in cautiously, as if she actually had a wounded heart; the hard knot that weighed so heavily in her breast seemed to have melted away; she breathed in again, this time more deeply. Then she raised one hand to her forehead and murmured: 'It's ridiculous . . . I think I'm a bit tipsy . . .'

'This light wine from Alsace is what you'd call deceptive,' said Jean-Paul.

With difficulty, Denise got to her feet.

'Let's go home, shall we, Jaja, it's late . . .'

He didn't protest, simply called for the waitress and paid the bill. But as they were driving back down the hill he suggested to Denise: 'Let's call in and say hello to Frédé . . .'

On the steep road, the small building that was the Lapin Agile looked decrepit, falling apart, like an eighty-year-old beggar. Age-old grime covered its walls.

At the end of the garden, which was planted with the spindly bushes you find at village inns, old Frédé was asleep on a bench; a tame magpie was pecking at some cherries left at the bottom of a glass of eau de vie.

'Let your friend sleep,' Denise begged. 'He looks so peaceful.'

They stood there, motionless. Dusk was falling slowly, almost reluctantly; an exceptional feeling of calm seemed to float over everything.

'This is just like the house of the good witch in German fairy tales,' said Denise.

An old clock chimed somewhere close by, slowly and solemnly marking the hour.

They left.

They picked up the car in front of the bistro. But they had hardly gone ten metres when it stopped. Jaja looked under the bonnet, then straightened up, swearing in despair.

'What's wrong?'

'It will take at least three-quarters of an hour to fix this,' he explained.

'But it's quite late,' said Denise, worried.

Jean-Paul thought for a moment.

'Never mind,' he finally decided. 'I'll leave the car with the owner of the café. He has a small garage. I'll come back tomorrow. We'll get a taxi home.'

But that was easier said than done. In the empty street, as quiet as a country lane, no matter how loudly they shouted, no taxi came. After ten minutes or so an old hackney cab happened to pass by, an ancient carriage teetering atop wide wheels, pulled along at a walking pace by a thin horse and driven by a coachman in a large greatcoat; both driver and horse had their heads lowered. In the evening light, amid the sleepy houses, the ancient carriage looked rather ghostly.

'Let's take it!' Jaja and Denise both shouted at the same time.

'It's like being back in the 1880s with Yvette Guilbert, the singer,' Jaja remarked, amused.

The coachman whipped the horse; the animal lurched a bit, which could have passed for an attempt to gallop, but soon slowed down again. The driver seemed to go back to sleep as well. Denise and Jaja, huddled together in the narrow carriage, didn't say a word. It was if they were being lulled to sleep; streets and squares seemed to approach very slowly, pass by, then disappear from sight; the street lamps shone brightly, then they were plunged into great swathes of darkness; the horse's hooves pounded the cobblestones.

Jean-Paul took Denise's hand. 'Are you asleep?'

'No.'

He kept her bare hand in his own. She didn't pull away. What was the point? A little later on he said: 'We're nearly there.' Then he leaned forward and kissed her wrist. She said nothing. He had often kissed her hand. But this time the kiss lingered, felt more insistent. She acquiesced as if she were in the midst of some disturbing dream that was none-theless rather pleasant . . .

The carriage stopped. He helped her get out, then said goodbye to her, calmly, just as normal.

'Goodnight, Denise, sweet dreams . . .'

'Thank you . . . you, too,' she said, making an effort to smile.

As soon as she got inside she called for her maid.

'Marie, did anyone call?'

'No, Madame, but there's a telegram for you.'

Denise grabbed it, her heart suddenly racing furiously: she recognised Yves's handwriting. There were only a few words.

> *Please forgive me for not having telephoned as promised but I was in such a dark mood that it was just impossible. If you're free tonight, though, please come round.*
>
> *YOUR Y*

Then, as a postscript, he had added: *Please don't be angry, my sweet little Denise.*

'That's right. When he deigns to call I have to go to him, and with a smile,' thought Denise.

She asked how Francette was, ate quickly and went out again.

'If Monsieur gets home before me, tell him I've gone to the cinema.'

Yves was smoking a cigarette, waiting for her. He had hardly done anything but smoke all week. Still no news from Vendômois. But by its very intensity his anxiety had almost burned itself out. Yves had recovered the laissez-faire attitude that was at the core of his personality. He vaguely hoped that some miracle would fall from the heavens to save him.

He expected Denise to question him, reproach him, to cry. He was surprised to find her very calm, indifferent and sweet, with an odd expression in her anxious eyes that he had never seen before when she looked at him. They made love. He clearly wanted to lose himself in her arms, wanted to forget everything; but she was cold, detached, as if she was fearful of something within herself, or within him. When she was about to leave he pulled her back, kissed her.

'Denise . . .'

'So you love me tonight, do you?' she asked with an odd little smile.

'Yes.'

'So I've been . . . a good girl?' she asked again.

'Very good,' he said glibly.

Then, in a more serious tone of voice, he added: 'I love you when you're like this, my darling; this is how I always want you to be . . .'

'Ah, so you're happy? You'll sleep peacefully tonight?'

He smiled. 'I think so . . . And you, my love?'

'Oh! I will too . . .'

'I'm glad . . . Goodbye, my darling.'

21

The next two days passed strangely quickly for Denise; Jessaint had telephoned to say he was staying in Étampes for a week. Every day around lunchtime, Jaja came and fetched Denise and they would set off in his sports car towards Versailles or Saint-Germain. They would fly like madmen down the sun-raked roads. Once they stopped for something to eat at Ville d'Avray, at the edge of a little round lake that shimmered pink in the dusk; another time it was on the expanse of green grass in Saint-Germain. Denise could see the growing tenderness in her companion's eyes; she could imagine his finely shaped, sardonic lips holding back the impassioned words he dared not speak, and that pleased her even more; it brought spice to those moments of her life, a taste that was strong and sharp. Yet she never stopped thinking about Yves for a moment; he seemed to lie deep within her, dormant, hazy and indistinct, like a veiled portrait, and that feeling gave her a sense of peace after such great weariness. Beneath the darkening sky, she and Jaja would head slowly back, their hearts full of the inexplicable happiness that accompanies beautiful summer evenings like a smooth, sweet ache. Then they would go home. And after eating dinner alone – when she would obstinately refuse to think about her husband – Denise would hurry over to see Yves. They said little. Denise was becoming the woman he had always wanted, docile and silent; he would bury his head in the warm hollow of her bare shoulder and lose himself in the exquisite night; she now knew how to stroke his hair without saying a single word.

On the third day, as Yves had not telephoned at the time he normally did, Denise asked Jean-Paul to come round. He rushed over at once. Denise realised that he had undoubtedly been waiting for a sign from her every day and a strange sense of pleasure, with a touch of cruelty, like the pleasure of a secret revenge, filled her heart. It was beautifully warm outside. Through the open window she could hear the peaceful voices of the concierges sitting on their doorsteps, chatting to each other from house to house, as people did in the countryside. Every now and then the honeyed scent from a bush in full flower in the garden below wafted up with the wind.

'Let's go to the Bois,' Denise urged. 'Wouldn't you like some fresh air?'

It had been unbearably hot all day. Denise had closed the shutters, and dozed almost the whole day on her bed; she had only changed out of her pyjamas for dinner. Her cheeks were still rosy and hot, like a small child who is waking up. Jean-Paul walked over to her; from the open neck of her light dress he could smell her own very sweet perfume: the fresh scent of young plants.

'With pleasure,' he said, agreeing, his voice rather husky.

A few minutes later they joined the stream of cars heading towards the Bois de Boulogne. The wide road was packed with them bumper to bumper; there was a smell of petrol, gas and dust. But as soon as they passed the Porte Dauphine, the cool air that swept over their faces seemed exquisitely pure by comparison. The night was dark and mild. Every now and then, when they passed one of the restaurants nestled in the woods, light poured out, along with the sounds of music, and then the large black patches of the great clumps of trees stood out once more against the paler sky. And now there was a smell of dewy grass and trees and the sweet scent of flowers coming from somewhere unknown. As darkness fell, however, a veil of mist formed above the lawns and even from the road. It was as white and opaque as milk. Denise and Jean-Paul stopped near the racecourse. They were fascinated: all around them, everywhere, flecks that looked as if they were made of smoke or delicate snowflakes rose slowly from the ground; the tops of the trees seemed to emerge from a sea of milk.

'Oh! It's almost like chiffon . . .' said Denise, holding out her hands to touch it, as if she were a little girl.

'A fairy's veil,' said Jaja, 'what do you think?'

He leaned in towards her and, very quietly, repeated: 'What do you think?'

'Don't,' she said softly.

She knew what was about to happen. Yet she didn't want to stop him . . . Tonight, did a kiss mean any more than a cigarette, a piece of fruit, a sip of cool water that seems to quench the thirst without really doing so? Like an echo from deep within her memory, she recalled certain words her mother had said, words that had stayed with her, dangerously insinuating themselves: 'He wasn't her lover . . . He was a friend . . . then, little by little, she began to enjoy it . . .'

'Don't,' she said again, even before he had tried.

He kissed her.

'Ah!' she said, then turned her head away several times. But his young, eager lips found hers.

'I love you, I love you so much,' Jean-Paul whispered instinctively, his voice heavy with emotion. 'If only you knew how much . . . do you love me?'

'No.'

After a moment's silence he said: 'I don't care.'

She heard him but without understanding. He pressed his lips to hers in a long, soft kiss, tasting her hesitantly, the way you try a piece of fruit you have never eaten before.

They hadn't noticed that a few cars had stopped around them; in more than one, no doubt, young couples like themselves, pretending to be watching the mist, were kissing each other, hidden by the darkness. But someone had the idea of playing a mean joke and aimed his headlights at all the cars where two people were so close together that they merged into one. Cutting through the fog, the harsh light fell straight on to Denise and Jean-Paul; in a flash, their faces, pressed against each other, appeared completely white in the glare of the spotlight. Denise, surprised, pulled away so quickly that her hat fell off on to her lap; at the same time she started shaking: she thought she had heard a stifled cry quite close to her. But the beam of light had already moved away, maliciously probing the shadows in other cars where you could hear women crying out in anger. Denise tried to see through the darkness that surrounded her, but in vain; she couldn't make out a thing; a taxi, alongside them, suddenly sped off and disappeared; the other cars followed suit, driving away in all directions.

'I must be dreaming,' thought Denise.

All of this had happened so quickly that her confused impressions dissolved almost immediately. They drove around the Bois once more and in a little side road, where it was cool, Jaja kissed her again. But when he moved his lips to kiss her cheek, on Yves's favourite place, she instinctively pulled away.

'No, not there . . .'

He looked at her in surprise.

'Let's go home,' she said curtly.

He obeyed, realising that her moment of weakness had passed.

As soon as she got home she called for Marie.

'Has anyone telephoned for me?'

'Yes, Madame,' the maid replied, 'Monsieur Harteloup.'

'How long ago?'

'Oh, quite a while; almost right after Madame went out.'

'Did he say anything?'

'No, Madame. He said he'd phone back tomorrow.'
'Thank you, Marie. That will be all.'

That evening, right after dinner, Yves had in fact telephoned her. When he heard the maid say 'Madame has just gone out' he was almost annoyed. Never in the eleven months of their affair had anything like this happened. Denise had always been there, at his beck and call, awaiting his pleasure, waiting to be summoned. He was ashamed at the frustration his disappointment made him feel, yet he couldn't manage to shake it off. He started pacing back and forth through his apartment, vaguely hoping there was some misunderstanding, that she would phone him back. But no. It was actually true. She wasn't there.

'Where the hell could she be?' he wondered. 'Her husband hasn't come home yet . . . Where is she?'

Then he thought better of it, made an effort to smile.

'This is a fine state of affairs . . . My poor Denise . . . Oh, good Lord, she's free to do as she pleases . . . If she started making a fuss like this every time I went out without telling her first, I'd be really irritated . . .'

But even though he talked like this to himself, or rather to Pierrot, which he usually did, as the dog sat there watching the flies buzz around the lamp, Yves could not calm himself down. He thought back to that day in Hendaye when she had been gone since morning and he had wandered around everywhere looking for her, from the Casino to the beach. And that same evening she had found him crying by the Bidassoa river . . . He didn't know why, but this memory was painful . . . He threw his cigarette across the room angrily; it sent sparks flying as it hit the marble fireplace.

'I'm going out, Pierrot.'

Pierrot wagged his tail.

Yves gave his ears a gentle tug to say goodbye and left.

Once in the street, he walked for a little while and ended up hailing a taxi to take him to the Bois de Boulogne. He thought he would go to the Pavillon Royal to get something cool to drink; but in the milky mist, the night was so extraordinarily beautiful that he told the driver to keep going until they reached Longchamp. And while he was there, in the darkness, a few cars came and parked alongside him, including a small open-topped convertible, where he could just about see a couple in each other's arms. He had been watching them for a short time when the harsh headlights from another car suddenly fell on them. Denise's face appeared just a few feet away from him; she was leaning back a little; a young man was kissing her; she was acquiescing and smiling.

All of a sudden he saw her push the man away. In the eerie white light he could see her hair with its curls blown by the night breeze, her delicate, sculpted face, her serious mouth and the beautiful, frank expression in her eyes that he loved and that stared at him through the darkness without recognising him.

And then, as if it had been a mirage, everything vanished.

The taxi was already heading towards the lake even though he was still standing up, stunned, both hands clutching on to the door of the cab. A sudden jolt when the taxi hit something as it turned a corner brought him back to reality.

'Stop!' he shouted. Then he got out, paid and started walking into the woods towards Longchamp. He had no particular plan; he was simply heading for the place where he had caught a glimpse of Denise, as if she might still be there. After a few minutes he stopped. 'I'm going mad,' he said out loud. 'She will have gone a long time ago.' Yet he continued walking aimlessly, knocking against the trees he couldn't see in the dark.

He experienced not a single moment of doubt. He did not wish to doubt. He never ran away from misfortune, but threw himself towards it at once, as if it were a frightening abyss that is both terrifying and enticing. Who was that man? He hadn't been able to see him. Just a young face with smooth, combed-back hair. Besides, that hardly mattered. So Denise was cheating on him, she was lying – Denise? He stopped, utterly defeated. Only now did he understand how rare, how extraordinary, how precious was the blind trust he had placed in her. But why? After all, she was a woman and, like all women, weak and a liar. Had she really been just 'any other woman' to him? Had she been a passing fancy, the memory of a beautiful summer's day, as so many others before? Had he not always treated her more or less like a wife? He had respected her for a long time, in Hendaye, as if she were a virgin. And ever since then had he ever knowingly offended her, even unconsciously, by suspecting the slightest word she said or a single thing she had done? The beautiful, frank expression in her eyes . . . But that, that was nothing . . . He might eventually have come to doubt her honesty, but her love for him? Never!

He had never even thought about her love. Does anyone ever think about something he possesses, something he believes he will always possess? Her love had been firmly rooted in his heart as a basic truth, a premise it was pointless to attempt to prove. He knew that she would never stop loving him, just as he knew that the earth would turn, that the sun would give light and that day would always, always, follow night. Like a sick child who lashes out against the people trying to make him well again, he could be harsh towards her, send her away: that was his right, she belonged to him. He knew absolutely that as long as he wanted her she would be there. This love had lit up his life like the softly caressing, hazy light from a lamp . . . Now, that light had gone out . . . Could he forgive her? The idea never even crossed his mind. What was the point? What he had loved in her was the security she gave him. Her beautiful eyes, her lips, her slim figure: other women were just as lovely, but he could never have trusted any other woman the way he had trusted her. So there was no point in trying . . . Denise was dead.

He stopped. He had wandered through the woods and ended up back near the lake. He walked over to it and stared at the water long and hard. The ripples made him feel slightly dizzy, almost slightly sick; the water moved and shone dimly. He left. He found himself outside the Bois. He walked along the deserted boulevard, then headed down a narrow street. Suddenly he felt weary. There was a wine merchant's that was still lit up. He went inside, sank down on a bench against the wall and ordered a drink from the bar. He was brought some wine. He emptied his glass in one go and refilled it. He almost felt like getting drunk. But the cheap wine made him feel sick. He put the glass down, leaned on the table and put his head in his hands. Some workmen sat at the counter, drinking. They were chatting to one another. He listened to them talk without understanding what they said. The sound of human voices made him feel better. He was struck by one particular word: 'Tomorrow'.

'Ah, yes, tomorrow,' he murmured.

All his problems weighed down on him like a high wall that comes crashing down. Tomorrow. No word from Vendômois. No money. Bills due to be paid in three days. The office he hated. Tomorrow. The terrible heat. And then, nothing . . . Not a glimmer of light. The darkness, the emptiness . . . All the possibilities of salvation he had imagined in case Vendômois did not come to his rescue were brushed aside with stubborn hatred.

'We're closing, Monsieur,' said the bartender.

He automatically stood up, paid and left. And then he walked some more, for a long time, wandering aimlessly. The night passed. Suddenly he looked up and recognised his house. Later on he could never explain how he had got there. He went upstairs. In the hallway, he knocked into something on the floor. He leaned over. It was a suitcase. Jeanne came out of the servant's pantry; she was still half asleep.

'Monsieur, there is a gentleman waiting for you.'

He pushed open the door. Vendômois.

As if in a dream, he heard him say: 'Hello there . . . Forgive me for not coming sooner . . . But I had to leave everything more or less in order back there, you understand . . . Then, as soon as I could, I hopped on a train . . . Things are clearer face to face than by letter, don't you think? And besides, I had some business to attend to in Paris this month . . . Why didn't I send you a telegram? Because there's no telegraph office in my little village buried in the snow. A letter would have arrived at the same time as me . . . But what's the matter? You look like a ghost . . . Don't worry, now . . . we'll sort everything out . . .'

Yves wiped his forehead with a trembling hand; all he could say was 'Thank you, thank you'; his voice was so blank that even he was surprised when he heard it.

'Are you all right?' Vendômois asked quickly.

'No, forgive me.'

'Is it just the money?'

'No, it isn't.'

Vendômois nodded. All he said was 'Ah'.

Yves smiled gratefully; this masculine restraint that silences even pity was exactly what he needed. He looked at his friend.

'Jean,' he said suddenly.

'Yes.'

'When are you going back?'

'Day after tomorrow, two o'clock.'

'Could you stay for two more days?'

'I could.'

He had looked up and was watching Yves carefully. Yves looked like a little boy who was about to cry.

'Jean, take me with you.'

Vendômois shrugged his shoulders. 'Of course,' he said.

22

That morning in July, Denise waited with feverish anxiety for everyone in the house to wake up so she could get dressed and go out without arousing suspicion. She hadn't slept a wink all night: her heart was filled with a horrible fear, and this time her anguish was, alas, all too appropriate. Another week had passed with no sign of Yves. At first she had thought it was quite normal. However, after a while his absence began to feel different to her. After waiting two days she finally decided to telephone him. For twenty minutes she listened to the phone ringing in the apartment. No reply. She phoned two or three times. Nothing. It was a mystery. She was about to go and find out what was happening when her husband came home. Throughout the evening she had not dared make a move. The night had been dreadful. 'He must surely be ill,' she thought. She remembered how terrible he had looked for some time now. Perhaps he had ended up in some hospital? My God, my God, if it were true that he was somewhere like that, in pain, hidden away in Paris, all alone in this big city, she would abandon everything in the world – her husband, her child – to run to him. Collapsed on her bed, she was tormented by a slow, subtle, obsessive form of torture . . . And this night that seemed to never end . . . At last it was morning. As soon as she heard her husband waking up in the room next door, his smoker's cough, then his voice, she rang for her chambermaid. Within a quarter of an hour she had washed, dressed and was in the street outside her house.

It was a stormy, oppressive July day. In spite of the early hour, a sickly-smelling mist was already rising from the overheated asphalt; the trees were losing their little yellow leaves; they were curling up, cracking, scorched by the heat. In the taxi, Denise gritted her teeth and clasped her burning hands together. The taxi stopped. There was Yves's house. Denise walked by the concierge's lodge with her head down, as she always did, and bounded up the stairs. She rang the bell. Its sound echoed sharp and clear. She waited. No one came. She rang again, longer this time. She could hear the shrill, panicky sound resonating throughout the rooms. But there were no footsteps, not even the sound of breathing from inside. She started banging her fists against the door. The concierge came running up when she heard the noise.

'Can I help you, Madame?'

'Monsieur Harteloup?' Denise whispered.

'He's gone, Madame.'

Denise stared at her wide-eyed, so the woman felt she should explain: 'He's left Paris.'

'Will he be gone for long?'

'Oh, yes! I think so . . . He's broken his lease. They're supposed to come and move the furniture out tomorrow.'

'Where did he go?'

The concierge either didn't want to say anything to avoid any problems, or she genuinely did not know. She just shook her head.

'You don't know?'

'No.'

'All right,' Denise murmured.

She was stunned, as if a bomb had fallen straight on her. It didn't even occur to her to insist, to force the concierge to break her silence with a large bribe. A distant memory flashed into her mind. When she was a very small child, she often had a dream that her father was dying; they were horrible nightmares that woke her with a start, all covered in sweat. Perhaps it was a premonition? Perhaps she'd overheard someone talking about his heart condition. In the end, he died suddenly, as she had seen twenty times over in her dreams; she remembered how that tragedy had left her dazed and resigned. 'It' had to happen. She had known that, on some level, for a long time. Now, standing outside this closed door, a similar feeling of fatality crushed her. Her anguish and worries, her frustrated need always to have her lover at her side, the despair that gripped her if he was away for two days, were not all these things a premonition of what was to come? – this silent door, the bell ringing in the empty apartment, this horrible helplessness that utterly overwhelmed her, here, on the sunlit landing, in front of this indifferent woman.

Without a word she started down the stairs, her shoulders hunched, as if someone had hit her very hard on the nape of the neck. At the bottom of the stairs she stopped. Her heart missed a beat. How many times had she put on her gloves, straightened her hat, powdered her face right here behind the large carriage doors before walking out into the street. And now she would never do that again, never again . . . She was surprised to hear herself groan out loud. But there was still one lucid thought in her mind. She wanted to know where he was. She hailed a taxi and was taken to his office. The director agreed to see her at once, for she had sent in her card; she was aware that he was staring at her in astonishment, but the thought of her outrageous behaviour in revealing her husband's name did not even bother her. The director was happy to tell her everything he knew. Harteloup had gone to Finland, suddenly called there, he believed, on family business; he had his address.

'Do you think he will be gone for long, Monsieur?' she asked in a breaking, poignant voice.

'He told me he wasn't ever coming back,' the director replied, somewhat hesitantly.

'Ah!' she said and stood absolutely still. But her cheeks had turned very pale and the corners of her mouth fell, suddenly making her look older.

'Would you like his address?' the director asked, embarrassed.

'Oh, yes! Please, Monsieur,' she said as if she were a little girl who believes she will get what she wants if only she is sweet and patient.

Indeed, she was given an envelope on which was written:

Savitaipole.
Commune of Koirami,
near Haparanda
(Finland)

And it was only when she read those strange words that she clearly understood how far away he really was.

The director looked at her with a mixture of pity and curiosity, vaguely expecting her to faint. But she suddenly regained her composure, as if she had been whipped.

'Thank you.'

He tried to mutter something sympathetic. She looked at him so strangely that he fell silent.

'Thank you, Monsieur.'

And, brushing past him, she left.

She was back in the street again, holding the bit of paper where Yves's address was written. She threw it far away. What was the point? Had she ever dared defy his will? And wasn't his will clearly obvious from the fact that he had gone without even saying goodbye? 'I've always known . . .' she thought once more, 'I've always known that he would leave one day without a word . . .'

In a daze, she headed towards her house; at the corner of the street she stopped: she recognised her husband's car parked in front of the door. She checked the time and was surprised: it was nearly noon. Soon she would have to sit down for lunch, sit down opposite Jacques, let him see her poor face ravaged by tears . . . She would never, ever have the strength to do that! The moment her husband asked her what was wrong she would burst into tears and confess everything.

She walked to the nearest post office and telephoned her house to speak to Marie.

'Marie, I won't be coming home for lunch . . . I've been delayed . . . I'm with a friend who isn't well . . .'

Leaving Marie to explain, she went outside. The horrible heat did her good: it prevented her from thinking, from remembering . . . She had almost stopped suffering; all she could feel was the asphalt burning her feet through her thin-soled shoes. She walked, just walked, unaware that she was perhaps retracing the tragic steps of her lover on a different night . . .

Without quite knowing how, she found herself on the quayside along the Seine. She crossed a bridge. Some cool air wafted up from the water. Suddenly her resignation, which was nothing more than a kind of physical numbness, dissolved in a rush of despair that made her stop dead and clasp her throat as if she were suffocating.

'Yves, Yves . . .'

She didn't judge him. She had always felt a mixture of incomprehension and superstitious respect for him that was almost the definition of how a woman loves a man. She felt neither hatred, nor bitterness, nor contempt. Simply immense astonishment. She did not even read into his disappearance any reason other than his masculine will that must be blindly accepted, like the will of God. She had not the slightest inkling of the truth. And besides, had she known, had she even suspected that Yves was alongside her that dark night in the Bois de Boulogne, she probably still would not have understood any more than she did now . . . Could what she had done been called 'cheating', a joyless game, a way to pass the time that had taken her mind off things for a few hours? Hadn't she really done it for him, in fact, to try to control the overwhelming love that obsessed her, was suffocating her? She certainly did not feel guilty where Yves was concerned. But she didn't really try to understand. When you are dying, you don't ask 'why?'. It's just inevitable.

She walked, simply kept walking, without feeling tired, vaguely comforted because she was alone, with no one there to whom she had to pretend, lie, smile.

She continued down the quayside. Every now and then her weary eyes closed against the sun's intense reflection off the Seine, then she breathed in the unpleasant smell of coal that rose up from the riverbanks. Parrots squawked inside a shop; the open doors of cafés offered a bit of shade, and little gusts of cool air, tinged with the smell of sour wine, wafted out.

Struck by a memory, as sudden and elusive as a certain scent, Denise stopped. She looked intently around her. She remembered. She had come here once, with Yves. Only it had been on a winter's evening, in the rain . . . Road workers in damp waterproofs were trying to warm themselves, holding out their hands over the red flames of a brazier, and they had laughed as she and Yves passed by: they walked past so serenely, holding each other close, in the rain . . . and the lights of the city had flickered as if the wind were about to put them out . . . Oh! She remembered, she remembered so well . . . And, as often happens, that memory led to others, like a line of children holding hands . . . She could picture Yves's face in haunting detail. She could see even further and deeper than his features – the expression in his eyes, his smile, his fleeting changes of mood, his pale, insipid desire, his anger, his weariness, his rare rushes of tenderness, his whims, his silences.

And then, in amazement, she also remembered how unhappy she had been. She couldn't understand any more. She carefully went through their entire affair in her mind. Monotony, boredom, anxiety, sadness . . . A wretched love, as grey and sad as an autumn's day . . . Why had it now been transformed in her mind into a bitter sweetness? Like a sick man who knows he is about to die and who tries to console himself by recalling his illness, his suffering, his miserable life, she tried once more, with a desperate effort of will, to call up the terrible times, the anguish, the doubts . . . But those thoughts were as faint and pallid as the dead. Then, suddenly, another memory – one she did not wish to recall – rose up, so clear and vibrant that she wanted to cry out. Yves's smile, his sweet, unexpected smile, as innocent and serious as a child's, that all at once lit up his face, then slowly faded away, leaving a fluttering light at the corners of his mouth. She saw him so clearly, so close by, that she instinctively stretched out both arms, as if she could touch him.

'But that was happiness!'

She had shouted it out loud. Men passing by looked at her in amazement. She felt ashamed. Her outstretched hands fell to her mouth, stifling her sobs. She stood there, coming to her senses, mortally wounded and exhausted, staring with a blank expression at the shimmering Seine. A taxi was passing; the driver saw her and slowed down. In a daze, she got in and gave her address.

The car drove on, jolting along the jagged paving stones of the old streets. She didn't cry. She wasn't even in pain any more. Like a little girl trying to work out a problem she doesn't understand, all she did was say again and again: 'So it's over, it's over . . . And I didn't even know that was happiness . . . And now, it's over . . .'

PREFACE TO THE FRENCH EDITION

Irène Némirovsky's first novel opens in a setting she knew well: Hendaye, where she spent her last holiday with her husband and daughters in August 1939, in one of those 'houses in mock Basque style' bathed in 'the scent of cinnamon and orange blossom', only steps away from a beach covered in 'warm sand'. Could anyone have believed that, beneath this 'August sky', the announcement of the German–Soviet Treaty would come to shatter all her hopes of finally being granted French citizenship? And how strangely this final confession of the abandoned mistress resonates: 'So it's over . . . And I didn't even know that was happiness . . .' Is such bitterness the price of twenty years of loyalty to a country for which she is first to declare her love in this book in such a moving way, a love that extends from the heights of Montmartre to the shores of the Bidassoa river. Even the youngest character in the narrative, the mischievous little girl, is called France . . .

But this is a mere illusion: for we are in August 1924, and there is no storm in sight to threaten the affair between Denise Jessaint, 'a young wife doted upon by a husband who earned a lot of money', and Yves Harteloup, a 'little rich boy' who was wealthy when he was young but who cannot bring himself to sacrifice life's luxuries in order to afford its necessities. All the elements of a love affair come together: a single man hoping to rediscover the 'beautiful mornings of his childhood', a 'very pretty' mother whose husband must go away on business, a deceptive sun that strips them bare and makes them forget their prejudices. A cold autumn rain will fall on this paradise, forcing Adam and Eve to cover themselves: he in a shabby business suit, she in 'silver shoes' and pearls. At the end of this on-and-off romance, exactly one year after emerging from the 'dazzling light of the Basque country', their love would suffocate in the 'horrible heat' of the Parisian summer. A match between a society woman and a man who was a member of what was already being called the 'new poor' could never work. If only they had known that every detail of their affair would be dissected under a microscope . . .

For even if *The Misunderstanding* appears to borrow some of the plot lines of a sentimental or melodramatic novel, this too is deceptive. Irène Némirovsky has no wish for the 'superficial poetry of some romantic novel' any more than Denise does. Tied into a 'kind of forgotten innocence', their romance becomes brutally subject to the harshest realities, confronted with the most trivial demands of everyday life. The glorious holiday by the seaside, worthy of a railway poster, is followed by a dismal post-war Paris. A young, exhausted hero crouches in the trenches of office work, while on the Avenue d'Iéna, a beautiful woman enjoys a life of leisure and is astonished to learn that her lover lives in an apartment in Pigalle with his dog . . .

With cruel determination, Irène Némirovsky distorts the fairy tale, brings the lovers back down to earth and constructs a 'border crossing that was . . . impossible to breach', made up of a hundred-franc note, the humiliation of a moment's pity, the torture of a silent telephone, the deep reluctance to give up modern comforts. Utterly destroyed by a sudden change of climate, Yves's and Denise's love decays under the attentive eye of the novelist until the moment when they become incapable of understanding one another: 'Can anyone really know anyone else?'

This disenchanted fable might be a variation on the theme of *L'Étape* by French novelist Paul Bourget, but it was in the name of social equilibrium that Bourget destroyed the fast-moving rise of his hero. Yves Harteloup, on the other hand, has dropped down the social ladder, and Irène Némirovsky is well aware of the fact that this '*mal du siècle*, but without the Romantic gloss' is the result of the damage caused by the Great War. Yves's education as the son of 'a pure-bred Parisian' made it inevitable that he would rub shoulders with the Jessaints; but having lost his fortune, his youth and his courage somewhere in Flanders, how could his class reflexes not lead to his downfall? Like 'Lazarus risen', had he experienced 'the horrors of death' only in order to follow Denise into a raucous nightclub filled with skeletons, toads and ogresses? In this luxurious cabaret, one might see the nightmare of Verdun merging with the 'cosmopolitan circuit'. And in fifteen years, having become cynical and corrupted and resembling the veteran Bernard Jacquelain (*Autumn Fires*), Yves Harteloup will grow richer with a clear conscience at the expense of this 'reprehensible and mad' world.

A '*trompe l'oeil*' sentimental study, *The Misunderstanding* addresses with astonishing acuity the psychological and social consequences of a war that Irène Némirovsky, still a teenager when it ended, would not see again until she witnessed the herds of people during the mass exodus from Paris in 1940. She wasn't yet twenty-three years old when this novel appeared under her name in *Les Œuvres libres* collection, in February 1926. And after the success of *David Golder*, four years later, this first novel was immediately republished. The critic Frédéric Lefèvre was right to marvel that such a young novelist had 'reflected on life enough to have a lucid and coherent vision of complex problems' (*Les Nouvelles littéraires*, 11 January 1930). Reflected enough, but also lived enough: Irène Némirovsky had experienced the Russian Revolution, exile and a lost childhood in St Petersburg, and had already learned one of life's lessons: happiness leaves a bitter taste, yet it 'was happiness' all the same.

Olivier Philipponnant
2010